In Those
Jeans

A NOVEL BY

CHANTEL JOLIE

Life Changing Books in conjunction with
Power Play Media
Published by Life Changing Books
P.O. Box 423 Brandywine, MD 20613

Library of Congress Cataloging-in-Publication Data;

www.lifechangingbooks.net

ISBN- (10) 1-934230847 (13) 978-1934230848
Copyright ® 2008

Acknowledgements

Truly giving God all the praise and worship for my health and strength, and for leading me in the right direction with my life. Without Him, I am absolutely nothing. You are the potter, and I am the clay, mold me Oh Lord.

A special thanks to my chocolate man for being patient and keeping me encouraged with my venture. 2008 has been great with you. These 12 years are magnificent. Yes, daddy.

A special thanks to my mother, Mary L. Green (baby doll) for teaching me that I can do anything that I put my mind to. To my father, Willie I. Bell Jr., who I enjoy having a good time with. You're a hoot.

Crazy mad love for Ms. Kimberly Goosby. Thank you for the connections. You are my girl for life – keep that hot bod. A special thanks to the House of St. James. You guys have truly been a blessing to me. Shout out to George Pinkard, the rags are fabulous. I have a great time wearing your creations. To Queen Burton, I love you so much. You taught me the art of being a grand girl, and stay true to thy self.

To Kevin Cummings, a hot designer. Alicia Todd (Lee Lee), Ms. Thang work it. You are a true inspiration to my life. Hold D-Town down, girl. Dr. Joy Rose, you have inspired me about education as we grow together in sequence. You have been a strong influence in my life.

To Tameka Robinson, thanks for the financial backing, my celeb beauty queen. A very special thanks to my clientele for supporting me as your hairstylist. You have been a family to me. To Stacy Gooden and family, you all treat me as an Anderson. Like an eagle I shall fly.

To my Publisher, Azarel (A Life To Remember, Bruised, Bruised 2 and Daddy's House), thank you for taking a lot of time and effort in schooling me about the business, and keeping a sense of humor with me. To Leslie Allen, I can't thank you enough for all the support, time and energy you have put into this book. To my publicist, Nakea Murray, thank you for all of your support. To Kathleen Jackson, thank you for doing the final editing. To Deshawn, The Ultimate Hustler, thanks for your support and the fabulous book cover. To the rest of my LCB family, you are all like family to me. Thanks for all the love and support.

Last, but never least, to my girl, Tonya Ridley, author of Talk of the Town, thanks for putting your trust in me, and guiding and supporting me. Without you, this book would've only been a thought, not a reality.

And to those that I didn't mention, please know that you are in my heart. Please look forward to Chantel Jolie's fleet of novels. This is not the end, only the beginning. I love all of you – friends, family and fans.

Visit the LCB guestbook at www.lifechangingbooks.net to post a comment or leave me a message about my book.

Smootches
XOXOXO

Chantel Jolie

Chapter One

I sashayed around the Savvy department in Nordstrom like I was the shit. Hell, all eyes were on me, or so I thought. With my new Gucci bag on my arm, I had to make room to throw just a few more high-dollar shirts across my shoulder. I was already loaded down and damn near out of breath from my quick strides. I had to hurry, 'cause a bitch needed money. This shopping spree was, unfortunately, out of necessity, not pleasure. If I didn't hurry up and get some clothes to sell, my ass would be broke…and I do mean bottom of the barrel broke.

Carlos, my Columbian Sugar Daddy, broke me down just last night when he told me our relationship was over. Done. Finito. I damn near lost my mind when he said he was sick of my shit. His facial expression showed he was one hundred percent done. He started throwing all my jewels around he'd gotten me, and even threatened to cut up my new fur coat. I remember thinking, *my fur*? *Oh, hell no*!

Carlos told me my new scheme, trying to get to Brazil for a new set of tits, was the last stop. He'd had enough. Especially when I told him what else I wanted to do to my body. I stopped for a moment, and pulled my arm close to my face. I loved Carlos' dirty draws. That man was my lover, my friend, my paycheck! I never had to worry about money, 'cause he laced my pockets on a regular basis. But the more I thought about his words, "It's over," the more ballistic I became.

While I was busy having a panic attack near the new

designer collection, I noticed from the corner of my eye, a thin, light-skinned chick with a long fake ponytail, staring me down real sly-like. She had on a Nordstrom name tag, but was just shuffling through the clothes like she was shopping too. She clocked me so hard, like she thought I was stealing. The nerve of that heifer, thinking I was a thief.

When I flipped my middle finger at that bitch, she turned her head quickly, like she didn't see me. At that point, I snatched two more Dolce and Gabbana sweaters off the rack and headed to the counter, swaying my perfectly shaped ass from side to side.

Just my luck, my stalker slid behind the register with an attitude, and swung that fake-ass ponytail like she was doing something big. That's how broads rolled in Detroit. Every last one of us thought we were the shit, and the world revolved around us.

"Honey, do you watch all your customers that closely?" I snapped.

She didn't respond, just shot me a nasty look. The moment I threw all my clothes on the counter, she started grabbing a few items, entering information into the register.

"I mean, I know I'm beautiful," I said loudly, turning around for her to see my well-formed shape. Hell, I'd worked hard on perfecting my body, and wasn't afraid to flaunt it. "Pray at night," I suggested to the bitch. "He might do something to help that pitiful shape of yours," I ended, with a snap and a sarcastic snicker.

I expected her to lose her cool, but she was still trying to win the employee of the month award. I knew there was no way in hell that I'd let a customer talk to me that way. I talked even more shit for the next three minutes, throwing insult after insult. Still in all, she never said anything negative, just kept ringing up piece after piece. That's why it shocked me when I finally heard her speak.

"That'll be $6, 442.52," she said, in a professional tone.

I whipped out my matching Gucci wallet, and combed through the many credit cards. I knew which one I needed to use. I was just showing off a bit.

After I handed the Visa to the woman, it only took a few seconds for her facial expression to change. Her eyebrows twitched and her lips did a funny dance.

"Ummm...I need to see some I.D."

"No problem," I snapped, with major attitude.

She stood back with her hands on her hips, waiting for me to comply. I flipped back open my wallet making sure she couldn't see inside. I had to find the I.D. that matched the stolen credit card I'd just given her.

My fingers touched the driver's license that read Chanel Martinez. *Oh shit, that's me*, I thought to myself. I scrambled even faster, looking for the right I.D. Suddenly, I saw it. Cynthia McBride. I grabbed it, handed it to the clerk, and smiled.

"Are you always so pleasant?" she asked sarcastically.

"It is what it is," I shot back and turned my head.

As the clerk validated my information, my thoughts wondered off. I thought about the three girls I had lined up to buy the clothes scattered across the counter. I had told them I'd meet them around five today, 'cause I needed the money fast. In all, I would make roughly $3,200.00 if I charged them half price for the clothes. They loved it when I came around with fancy, hot off the press shit. Three more stops like this today, and I'd have the rest of the money needed for my trip. I breathed heavily, thinking back to how I resorted to identity theft again.

I was able to give up that lifestyle after meeting Carlos, who catered to my every need. Luckily for me, I kept in touch with my old contacts. So the moment I told my girl,

3

Cheryl, I needed to get hold of some high-limit credit cards, she was on it. Cheryl was from Detroit, and made millions of dollars running credit card scams and stealing other folks identity.

I remember trying to get close to her, to get some extra perks, but she wasn't having it. It was strictly business. Pay her for use of the cards, then lose her contact number after that.

My attention was diverted when I heard the static noise of a walkie-talkie behind me. I looked over my shoulder to see what the commotion was all about. Suddenly, it dawned on me that something was up. The woman who was waiting on me, wore a grin that said payback. I wondered what she really had on me. Did she know the credit card wasn't legit? Or did she find out the license was a fake?

"Miss, we need you to come with us," a tall, slender gentleman said to me, standing about two yards to my left. He was dressed in casual attire, with a pair of tan khakis that drooped to the floor.

I wasn't exactly sure who he was, but I wasn't going anywhere with his ass. I looked at him intently before speaking, and noticed his high top fro.

"No, the hell I'm not," I barked. "I'm just waiting on my bags." I turned and looked at the woman like everything was okay. I stood firmly like I was calling the shots. "Can you finish bagging my stuff, 'cause I gotta go."

The woman crossed her hands, and leaned back on the counter with another smirk on her face. I knew I had to make a move. I peeked over my shoulder once again to figure out my options. Two guys stood outside the perimeter of the department that I was in. Another stood close to the entrance into the mall. The only man close enough to be a problem was this guy looking at me with the high top fro. But luckily, he was a slender brotha and could be handled. I was 5'9, and equipped to rumble if necessary. I'd been lifting weights, keeping my body toned, so my money was on me.

I turned one last time ready to leave my investment on the counter. With a quick two-step in the direction of the front door, I barged through what was headed my way.

Someone yelled into the walkie-talkie, "Suspect is on the move!" That's when I knew they would be all over me.

For a second, I contemplated stuffing a few shirts in my purse. Hell, I was already in trouble. In record time, I dashed past a few racks, knocking down several pieces of clothes in the process. One woman, who was pushing her daughter in a stroller, looked at me strangely. She must've thought I was crazy the way I was dodging the men who I now assumed were security. Too many times my mind told me to switch positions. I dashed out one way, then turned and headed another, so confused, I didn't know how to escape. They moved closer. I stepped back. Finally, they had me cornered.

I glanced over my shoulder, only to see a wall filled with shelving and neatly folded jeans. I glanced to my left at the two short men, who looked just as scared as me. To my right, stood the most aggressive looking guy of them all, my friend with the fro. His eyes met mine fiercely. He was determined to take me in.

"We just need to take you downstairs to our offices to talk," he said sincerely.

"For what? I didn't do nothing," I stated adamantly.

"We know. We just gotta clear some things up. Come with us," he replied, in a more welcoming tone.

He turned his back toward me, and gave me the eye like he wanted me to follow him on my own. I wasn't sure what they really knew, so I figured I would comply.

As I followed, the three other guys immediately got behind me and followed closely. We all walked together in a pack, but way too damn close if you ask me.

By now several customers had gathered around, and clearly thought I'd been caught stealing. The looks and stares had me feeling guilty.

"Close your eyes, sweetie," one white woman said to her daughter.

"What the fuck you looking at me for?" I belted. A few jerked back and turned the other way, but most continued to stare.

When we entered the security office, my four escorts stopped abruptly at the door. They all had confused expressions, like they weren't sure what was going down. I tried to play it cool, but my stomach churned inside.

"Go get the merchandise from the sales clerk," the head man requested. "I'll call the police," he said to the others, just before slightly pushing me inside a small office. When I heard three deadbolts on the door make a clicking sound, my heart dropped down to my shoe. I was floored. I had been tricked! My bulging eyes looked desperately for an escape, but none were near. The small cement wall room was perfect for detaining thieves like me. My mind flashed to a picture of a jail cell. *Oh...hell no*, I thought. Jail definitely wasn't meant for somebody like me. I wouldn't stand a chance.

I fell down into the wobbly chair, ready to black out. Clearly, I needed oxygen.

"You alright Miss," the security officer asked.

I couldn't respond.

***

Twenty minutes later, my hands were cuffed and behind my back, while being led to a Detroit city police car. A single tear fell from my eyes at the thought of not reaching my goal. I'd done all this just to earn enough money for my trip, and now I truly wasn't gonna make my flight to Brazil tomorrow. It's all I really wanted in life.

The city police officer who held me by my arms didn't have any remorse for me. I batted my eyes and did my usual flirting that I did with men, but nothing worked. He was straight by the book, and being freed by him was out of the question. Finally, his last words hurt me deeply.

"You might be going away for a long time, baby girl," he smirked.

I wanted to snap back with my favorite line, *it is what it is*, but decided it was too perfect for what was about to happen to me.

Chapter Two

Three Weeks Later

What was supposed to be the happiest time of my life turned out to be the most emotional and chaotic. I sniffled a little, ready to drop a few more tears, then caught myself as the skinny stewardess walked by. She wouldn't even allow me to be upset in peace. What the fuck? She had been all in my business since the flight left Brazil five hours ago. The bitch kept asking me all kinds of personal questions. How was my trip? Why was I there? Was it my first time?

Then she hit me with another question. "Did you get any fabulous clothes?" she asked, kneeling to get closer in my face.

I started to tell the bitch, *'No...but I did get these tits!'* Maybe if I pulled up my shirt and flashed her ass with my new double D's, she would leave me alone. I guess she was just being friendly, but she was way too happy, talking to majority of the passengers. "No," I finally said, in the most hostile voice I could muster.

Miss Gurl shot me another annoying smile. The little bitch had the cheery personality thing going that I was supposed to have. My life was supposed to be perfect by now. Instead, I sat in my tight airline seat, crying inside, 'cause I had nowhere to go, no one to call, and was wondering why in the hell I was in this situation.

When the stewardess walked away, it gave me a chance to think about my crazy life. Three weeks ago I was let out of jail on bail, and quickly rounded up enough money to make it to Brazil. I called in a few favors, and performed a few stunts for one of my old heads. Finally, I'd put together enough cash for my trip. Of course I wasn't supposed to leave Detroit, but who would know. My stupid-ass court appointed lawyer said my court date wouldn't come up until next month. So, I figured I would find me a new Sugar Daddy this week, or at least convince Carlos to give me some money for a sharp lawyer; one who would get those wack-ass credit card fraud charges dropped. That would be the least he could do since he'd been ignoring my damn calls.

I leaned back in my seat, wondering what I would do when the flight landed. The course was Hot-Lanta, but what part of Atlanta was the mystery. I had no idea where I'd lay my head. There were no men with money lined up, no family I could call, and no friends who would reach out to lend a hand. Nothing! No one!

A phone call to my mother back in Detroit wouldn't even help. She and my father had disowned me a while back. So, asking them for even a dollar would result in zilch-zero-nada. I couldn't blame them though. Most people couldn't handle what I had done. Most who knew me well, said years ago, it was a disgusting, pure betrayal to my family. My mother still loved me though… I knew it in my heart. Although a grown woman, pushing twenty-eight, I was still *her* baby.

The last time we saw each other face-to-face, she just shook her full head of grey hair with worry. I wanted to reach out and hug her tightly, but knew she would see straight through me. She always did have mother's intuition when it came to me. She knew exactly what was going on all along, but hid it from my father as long as she could. I hadn't seen them in two years, so they wouldn't know me if they saw me.

I thought deeply about my family. Overall, we were what people call super dysfunctional. We've buried so many secrets that Jerry Springer, Oprah and Tyra should be fighting to book us on their shows.

Finally, hearing the captain say, "Flight attendants, prepare for landing," was somehow scary for me, and snapped me from my daze.

I was ready to get off and stretch my long legs, yet the sense of the unknown had me shaking all of a sudden. I grabbed my purse, pulled out my diamond encrusted compact mirror and applied my favorite Mac lip gloss. My gloss always seemed to give me a sense of peace; maybe even security. Most people hated that my behavior was always so girlie-girl, but I loved feeling like a sexy woman.

I smiled, smacked my lips and thought about my hair. My weave was tight, the best money could buy. Shit, $500.00 Remy hair straight from Malaysia to be exact, so all I had to do was fluff it a bit, to make sure it was in place. The part straight down the middle marked me with the Pocahontas look. Not to mention the fact that my perfectly trimmed ends touched the tip of my lower back.

When the jet door to the plane opened, I walked off slowly, hesitant about what was waiting for me in the big-bad-world. Any person in their right mind knew I had a lot brewing in my lil' head by the way I ignored everyone who said their goodbyes.

"Thanks for flying with us," the pilot said, with a smile.

I didn't even look at him. Nor did I say anything. I kept stepping in my thigh-high Ostrich skin boots, glassy eyed and all.

"Damn, sexy…don't hurt 'em," one man blurted out, when I stepped into the airport terminal.

I ignored him too. That was the effect I had on most men. I had mastered the strut of a run-way model years ago, which accented my voluptuous frame; so most men eyeballed

11

me boldly, while others took a sneak peek right in front of their women.

"Damn, Miss Lady, you got a moment?" a heavy-set brotha stopped to ask me.

I looked at his blinged out watch, thinking he might be the Sugar Daddy I was searching for. I huffed up a fake smile, and lifted my shoulders high so my new boobs could greet him properly. "I'm not sure. Why?"

"'Cause you the prettiest babe I seen all day."

"It is what it is," I responded.

Just as planned, his mouth opened and he started salivating like a dog after a piece of meat. "I was thinking we could get together later. You live here or just visiting?"

"Ahh…" I stuttered. "Why, you FBI?"

He laughed. "Nah…far from it. Why you say that?"

"'Cause, you sure do ask a lot of questions." I switched my carry-on bag over to my right arm, and threw my free hand on my hip, ready to find out more about the potential playa, I asked, "So, where you headed? You flying out?"

"Nah…I'm headed to work. I run the conveyor belts down in baggage claim," he proclaimed proudly.

What the fuck? Oh hell naw!

My neck rolled backwards and I stomped off, taking short disappointing steps, leaving the brotha standing in the middle of the floor. I couldn't believe he thought I was gonna lower my standards and hang out with a broke dude. I was already busted, and was doing a great job at being broke by my damn self.

About three yards down the corridor, the baggage claim sign reminded me about my two bags that I'd checked. I panicked, thinking if I had forgotten those, that would be the end of me. The only clothes I owned were in those bags.

I jetted down the steps as quickly as I could, headed to

Baggage Claim #10. When I got there, I breathed a sigh of relief. My two large Louis Vuitton duffel bags were just coming
around the conveyor belt. I grabbed a roll cart, plopped my
bags on the ledge, and headed to the pay phone.

The average person woulda thought I was just plain
nasty by the way my purse looked inside. I rambled around,
beneath, and in between my razor blade, panty liners, mace,
tons of credit cards, *all with maxed out balances of course*,
and my cell phone that Carlos had turned off weeks ago. Finally, a lil' change touched my fingers.

I whipped the coins from my purse, and slowly slid
them in the slit of the pay phone. My heart thumped as my
forefinger pressed each number. What would I say to convince him to forgive me? How would I ask him to send me
some money Western Union? Or for that matter, how much
would I ask for?

When the operator's voice sounded, I lost my breath
for a moment. *"The number you have reached has been dis-
connected."*

I stood dumbfounded. Carlos really wanted me out of
his life. I tried to remove what I thought was an imaginary
knife from my back, so I could get focused. I didn't have a
plan at all. Sadly, I placed the phone back down, and turned
around to walk away.

The sign above read "Taxi Cabs," so I headed in that direction. By the time I'd walked out of the airport, and hopped
into the back of a cab, everything had become clearer. I
looked like I belonged on Rodeo Drive, yet one hundred and
two dollars was all I had to my name.

My stomach cramped a bit once in the cab. I wasn't
sure if it was because the driver asked where to, or because I
was still spotting.

"Where can a girl make money in this town?" I asked
the cab driver.

13

The dirty looking Lebanese man looked at me strangely through his rear view mirror. "What kind of money?"

"Quick money," I responded.

"You a stripper."

"Not at all. But I gotta do what I gotta do, honey."

"I know a spot. But it's far out. Gonna cost you about thirty dollars. But you'll make money for sure. Gotta let people know what you offering."

I tapped on the seat twice, signaling him to hurry. "Let's go," I instructed, leaning back into the seat.

***

Thirty minutes later, we pulled up to a dirty looking spot in Cabbagetown. It was a side of town that I'd never heard about, and I knew why. No doubt, I didn't belong. I stood out like a sore thumb when my long legs swung from out of the cab. My driver darted around to the trunk, collected his pay, and zoomed off, leaving me and my bags resting on the curb.

"Hey, pretty lady," a tricked out guy shouted from the stoop, near the front door.

I turned to look at the beady-headed man sitting underneath the blinking sign above. *Jaycee's* it read. Damn. I thought about how the cab driver mentioned that the guys who hung at Jaycee's spent plenty of money, but there was a price to pay. They were dirty, sometimes funky, and real grimy.

By the time I got inside, I had swallowed my pride, knowing this would be my only way to collect some money for a hotel and food for the next few days. I weighed my options. I could either be aggressive, and go for the guy who looked like he had the most loot in the room, or find me a nice table and sit like a damsel in distress waiting for someone to approach me.

The first idea sounded better, so I walked the dimly lit room, and found a corner near the back to sit my bags down. However, before I could even get situated, an older man in his late fifties asked me if I wanted to dance.

"How much you paying?" I asked boldly.

"Damn, Momma. You belong on the stage over there. Look so good, I wanna sop your ass up with a biscuit. "

I thought, *this negro is country and corny as hell*. I glanced to where he was pointing, thinking a strip move was beneath me, but I needed money fast.

I repeated myself, "So, like I said. How much you pay-ing?"

"I got seventy-five."

"Oh, you real funny. Seventy-five what? Hundred?"

"That's seventy-five dollars. Take off the extra zeroes." He smiled widely.

"Honey, you can save that shit."

Before I could whisk him away, another gentleman ap-proached, and lifted his glass in the air for a toast. Problem was, where was my damn, drink? When I noticed the dia-mond stud shining brightly from his ear, I knew he was it.

"C'mon over here," I summoned, letting my old friend know he was done.

Just as my broke prospect got up to leave the table, my new diamond stud man made his way to the table and asked, "What's a Beyonce look-a-like doing in a place like this?"

I grinned, thanking him with a smile for his comment. In all honesty, people had always told me we resembled one another, especially with my tiny waistline and bootyliscious ass. I just didn't have her money or paid-ass Jay-Z on my arm.

Besides, my complexion stood out more. My honey-colored skin-tone came compliments of my biracial father. He was partially of Spanish descent and broke me off a tiny piece of his rich looking skin.

"Look, I ain't gonna front. I need money," I finally said. "I'm fresh off the plane looking for a good paying gig."

"Well you in the wrong place, sweetheart. You look like you got good taste," he continued, eyeing me up and down. "You belong up in Magic City."

"Magic City, huh?"

"Yeah…" He nodded and slid his hand up the side of my thigh.

I didn't tell him I'd already heard about Magic City. I just needed him and his pockets for the night.

"I'm gonna go there tomorrow. But for now, what's up with you, playa?"

"Who me?"

"Yeah you?" I asked, looking at a nicely dressed woman who walked past. She looked at me hard, like she wanted me. *Damn, I know I'm desperate when every woman and man in here is starting to look like dollar signs*, I thought.

"Look, baby girl, I'm married."

"So."

"So, I can't afford to catch shit. Lip service is what I'm looking for," he blurted out, then stuck a toothpick in his mouth.

I paused for about thirty seconds. Neither one of us said anything.

Then I asked, "How much?"

"Two hundred."

I wanted to say "No Deal," but what choice did I have. Instead, I uttered, "Let's do it."

Before I knew it, I was being led to a dark room way in the back of the club. The lights got darker the further we went. Suddenly, we stopped near a small janitor's closet. When the door opened, I knew I had to make an impression over at Magic City 'cause this shit wasn't gonna cut it.

Chapter Three

A loud banging sound woke me from my peaceful sleep. Exhausted was an understatement. In total, I'd only slept about sixteen hours over the last few days, and could've killed whoever knocked like a crazy person outside my hotel door. I threw the pillow over my head to drown out the annoying knocks, but the perpetrator wouldn't stop. Finally, I jumped from the squeaky bed, and looked for my pants that had fallen behind the outdated wobbly chair.

Nobody knew where I had decided to get a room last night, so figuring out who it was had me puzzled. Then it hit me, maybe my trick from last night couldn't get enough of my suck game, so he came looking for me? I smiled slightly. Any money was good money right about now.

I headed to the door, and pulled the heavy flowery curtain back a little for a quick view.

"Open the mufuckin' door," a dark-skinned woman shouted.

I couldn't see her face good, but the heaviness of her hands had me in shock. Who would've thought a woman could knock like the damn police. I opened the door slightly so I could ask a few questions. Instead, a raging woman burst through the door like it was a fucking drug bust. She brushed past me, looking into the bathroom, I guess to get a quick view of who was inside with me.

Her finger started pointing and moving back and forth like she was talking to a toddler. "It's one o'clock, and in case you didn't know…check out was at eleven."

I rubbed my eyes for a sec. Didn't say too much, 'cause the broad had me mesmerized. She was short, sassy, and shapely just the way I liked my women; one of those around-the-way-girls, scraggily ponytail and all.

For years, I'd been trying to shake my lust for women, but couldn't. Whenever I saw a woman who attracted my attention, I wanted to grab her by the lips and suck her dry. Ms. bad-ass wasn't good-looking in the face, but her body was built and tight. However, despite her banging body, she still needed her ass kicked, 'cause she wouldn't stop ranting.

"This ain't the Ritz Carlton, damn it. We're a small, black-owned company, and need this room cleared now, to rent to the next trick!"

I wanted to jump on her ass for that comment, but just stared at her instead.

"You on drugs or something?"

I shook my head. I needed to shake my mixed emotions and just cement a dick on my brain.

"Get your shit and get out," she demanded.

"Yeah, I hear you," I finally said. "You going too fuckin' far with your demands."

The twitching in my nipples snapped me back to reality. They'd been doing that over the last few days; a twinge here and a twinge there. Thankfully, the aches and hard pains had gone away over a week ago, but this was different...something strange.

I massaged my breast right in front of my new enemy. She just looked at me, walked toward the door, and tapped her watch. "Ten minutes," she ended, walking out.

I threw my pillow at the closing door. That bitch was treating me real foul, and for some reason, I was tolerating it. I had to shake this weakness for bitches, I told myself. I thought about her ten minute threat and headed to the bathroom to get ready, and gathered my shit. My next move would take some careful planning.

***

By the time I hopped into the cab, my confidence was back. I'd spent the last three hours pumping myself up, and repeating what I would say to the manager over at Magic City. I had even made a peace treaty with Ms. Billy-bad-ass before I left, who formally introduced herself as Stacy.

When I walked into the front lobby sporting my best skin-tight pencil skirt, long see-through shirt, and a Versace belt wrapped around my waist, Stacy just held her jaw low, wondering how I'd transformed into a Kimora Lee Simmons wanna-be. I lied and told her that I was in town to do an independent movie, and just needed a place to lay my head. Impressed and slightly star struck, Stacy apologized for bursting in on me.

She ended up being cool, but not cool enough, 'cause when I asked her to keep my luggage until I came back, the bitch said she was charging me $10.00. I thought, *shit, my Louie V gives this $49.00 a night dump an upgrade, so it should be free.* I left when she told me where I could get a bite to eat, and that there would be a late fee if I didn't pick up my bags by midnight when she got off. I just laughed it off, and told her every last pair of my boots better be in place when I returned. I mean, I loved all my clothes, but I was a crackhead for boots, and usually rocked them everyday.

The cab driver's voice snapped me from my thoughts when he said, "Here we are."

I glanced at the lot, noticing there were only five to six cars parked. But it was no surprise to me when a candy apple red Ferrari F430 stood out. I was a sucka for nice cars. Then I looked to my left at the sign raised high in the air that read, *Magic City.* Instantly, I got nervous. I'd worked at two different strip clubs back in Detroit right before hooking up with

Carlos, so I knew there was nothing to it. But Magic City had a reputation of employing the best girls the city had to offer. Besides, every baller, entertainer, and man with a money bag came through Magic City when in the ATL. I prayed that the manager would recognize good talent, and hire me on the spot.

"Don't hurt 'em too bad tonight, sexy," the cab driver stated, when I handed him the money.

I smiled slightly. "I'll try."

When I walked in, a funky aura filled the air, and the mixed loud sounds were nerve-racking. A woman was vacuuming in the middle of the floor with her head downward, while the sounds of R. Kelly's '*Sex Me*', competed with the noises. I looked around for someone who would know who I needed to talk to for a job, but everyone looked like they were on the move, preparing for a busy night.

The décor was real romantic–like. Leather couches, velvet cloth chairs, the whole nine. I walked around a lil' more until I finally spotted a gentleman sitting alone in a private section behind a sheer curtain. The area where he sat was sort of secluded and elevated about three feet from the floor. His face wasn't clear, but the way he puffed on the cigar, I just knew he'd have cancer by the end of the night. I headed in his direction, thinking he had to be the manager by the way he was suited up all professional and shit.

Suddenly, a woman appeared from behind the bar. "Hmmm…Hmm. Can I help you? We're not open yet?"

"Oh, I was just looking for the manager."

"For what?" the woman replied, with a smirk.

"He told me to come by for a job." I stuck my chest out and swung my hair just a bit. The confidence thing would always get me over.

"Big Willy in the back," she replied, and pointed to a narrow hallway in the far back corner of the room.

I headed that way, as the man sitting in the V.I.P section watched me like a hawk. I kicked it up a notch and switched hard on my way to meet Big Willy.

When I neared the end of the hallway, a gold plated sign hung from the door that said '*Office*'.

As soon as I knocked one time, a loud voice sounded, "C'mon in."

I swung the door open and produced the sexiest pose possible.

"You here about my liquor license?" the big, black thick beard man asked from behind the desk.

"Hell no. I'm here to see Big Willy."

"Why? You police?"

"Do I look like I'm here on police business?" Before he could speak, I continued. "Hell no. I need a job. I hear he the man."

I prayed that the slob behind the desk was Willy. I had a way with fat men; always knew how to make them feel like they were on top of the world.

"Damn. C'mon in then and shut the door. What's yo name, sexy?"

My finger pivoted quickly in the air, letting Mr. No-Name know that I wasn't talking to anybody who couldn't make power decisions. "First, are you Big Willy?"

He laughed like it hurt him to chuckle. "I like you already. Yes…yes, I'm Big Willy. Now, your turn."

"Chanel Martinez."

"Nah, yo stage name. I ain't got no interest in yo government shit."

"Oh…Ahh…," I hesitated. "Oh, Sparkle," I announced.

"Umh. You danced before?"

"Hell yeah. I'm from Detroit. Lemme show you how we get down."

I hopped up, threw my right leg up on the chair and started grinding. His eyes told me that he was sincere, all about making money, no games.

"Yo, I'ma give you a shot, but I don't tolerate no shit, 'cause you see my man Big Earl, he holds it down." He pointed with his over-sized pinky finger.

I turned around looking for Big Earl, but didn't see him. Then I noticed he was talking about the black .45 Caliber handgun resting low in the palm of his hands.

"All crooked bitches get hurt. Understood?"

Before I could respond, Big Willy immediately turned his attention to a 50-inch plasma TV on the wall and started yelling. "Now, that's what the fuck I'm talking about, nigga!" His hands looked like they stung from how hard he was clapping.

"Yeah, that was a nice assist. LeBron James is the shit."

Big Willy looked surprised. "So, you know a little something 'bout the game, huh? Most bitches don't know shit about sports."

"Who doesn't? LeBron is the best forward in the league. Averaged twenty-seven points a game last season."

He displayed a huge smile. "I like you already. Come with me."

Big Willy stood straight up, and for the first time I noticed that he was damn near 350 pounds. I followed his slow, wobbly-ass in awe out the door, toward the dressing room where his girls got dressed. When we entered, I thought, *trifling*. A pair of dirty red thongs greeted us at the door.

"Didn't I tell y'all bitches 'bout keeping this place clean? What the fuck?" he asked.

I couldn't figure out who he was talking to because there was only one girl in sight, and she was busy gluing some tracks in her hair. I laughed, but he was right, the room was nasty. It reminded me of the back room in the movie,

'*The Playas Club*'.

"This where you come tomorrow night. I'll have my girl, Lisa, here ready to help you get set up. Pick a station," he announced, looking at the long mirror lined with chairs in front. "And Chanel…"

"Yeah," I answered.

"Have a better mufuckin' stage name when you start tomorrow night."

"No problem."

Big Willy turned away from me like our short meeting was over. I had to quickly catch his attention. "Ahh…Willy."

"What is it?"

"Do you think I can get an advance?"

"Do you think you can get yo trick ass outta here." He never looked back, just snickered and talked shit on his way out the room, leaving me looking stupid. "Advance my ass. We don't do that shit in the Dirty South. We ain't even gon' start no shit like that. Everybody gotta work for theirs."

"No problem," I responded to his back-side. I sucked it up, and walked out of the dressing room like a champ. I held my head high, even though my pockets were low. Real low.

By the time I made it back out front, my senses told me that I was being watched. I scanned the room from the corner of my eye, only to see the same mystery man sitting behind the sheer curtain, still puffing his cigar. A waitress entered his secluded area, and bent slightly to hear what he had to say. Within seconds, the woman was out, standing near the red velvet rope, and flagging me down.

My fingers pointed to my chest. "Me?" I questioned.

"Yeah…you. You scared of money," she asked sarcastically.

Scared…Hell no. As bad as I needed money.

When I slipped past the waitress, she rolled her eyes, but I didn't give a shit. I guess she wanted me to stop by the rope and wait for permission to enter. I wanted to see what the brotha was working with. I strutted up on the platform where he sat, and pulled the curtain back. If I didn't know better, I would've thought I was in somebody's living room. The plush sofas and chenille fabrics gave off that type of vibe.

"You call for me?" I decided to ask, 'cause Mr. Mute just sat in silence and never stopped puffing.

He extended his palm, offering me a seat.

I sat in the chair directly in front of him, and stared him down boldly. He was dressed in true southern fashion, in what looked to be a royal blue suit. Being a true fashion connoisseur, I shook my head to keep from laughing. But, as broke as I was, he could've been dressed in a brown paper bag, and I wouldn't have cared. Besides, everything about him said money, so I was game for whatever he had in mind.

"So what's your name, sexy?" I let my foot rub up against his leg.

No response.

At that point I really started to think he was a mute. "Do you talk?" I asked, in a more aggressive tone.

"Shhhh," he said softly.

Suddenly, he pulled a thick stack of hundreds from his pocket and peeled off three bills. When he sat them on the table, he pushed the crisp bills my way and allowed his eyes to lock-in on mine for a moment. They seemed to avoid me, like he was hiding something. But they also seemed to ask me a question. I just didn't know what.

"Do I need to say more," he finally spoke.

I almost fainted, realizing he actually said more than one word.

I turned to look all around me. I could see through the curtains that more people were entering and exiting the club. I knew they could see a silhouette of me, just not my facial features clearly. *Hopefully Big Willy won't mind if I start a little early.*

"Where do you suppose we do this?" I turned back around to ask my milk-chocolate mystery man.

He just patted the arm of the sofa where he sat. That told me he wasn't interested in moving. The change in the volume of the music side-tracked me. Adina Howard's '*Freak Like Me*,' came blaring through the speakers, like it was my theme music.

Fuck it, I'm down, I thought. I hopped up, walked over to my mystery man, and threw my legs across his mid-section, straddling him with aggression.

My heavy hands cupped his cheeks and lower jaw with force. I wanted the muthafucka to say something. He didn't. So, I licked his neck with two long strokes of my tongue. He didn't show any emotion, so I slid back, unbuttoned his pants, and licked his dick the same way.

"Ahh…" he moaned, letting me know he was pleased.

His dick was short, but chunky. I grabbed it, stroking it hard, trying to make it grow. Mr. Mute twitched the more I stroked. The negro started drooling, so I knew the nerves in his dick worked well. Suddenly, he pushed me away slightly, just enough to let his pants drop to his knees. I followed suit and lifted my skirt, then cocked my thong to the side.

For some reason his silence was turning me on. I threw my head back at the feel of my clit caressing his dick. He made me act a little crazy, 'cause he gave me so much power. In full control, I knew I had to fuck him good, so he could be one of my regulars.

Out of the blue, I surprised him and slid my hand underneath, to insert his dick into my wet treasure. I got crazy at the feel of his warm rod, and grinded like a mad-woman. My forceful thrust had me thinking I was riding a sick bull, who couldn't move. I glanced at his face to see if he was enjoying it, and the confirmation came quicker than expected. He moaned slightly, flashing his chipped tooth dead in the front of his mouth.

"Oooooooohhh," he stuttered. "Yes…yes…yes…"

He finally started participating, swinging his waist and upper hips into me. I pounded back like I was the man. I liked feeling like the dominate one; always did. It was in my blood.

"Work that shit, Momma!"

He grabbed my hips and pulled my body forcefully into his, and then away from him repeatedly. In and out he dove. I could tell he was about to explode, so I grinded harder and harder, meeting his every thrust. Suddenly, his body shook like a big vibrating pager.

I leaned over and whispered in his ear. "Honey, I should get a few extra dollars for that."

Again, he went back to being a mute as I wiped the sweat from his forehead and got up. I watched as he pulled his pants back up and went into his pockets to hand me another three hundred. I smiled to show my gratitude. I thought, damn, *he paid well, but his personality was too damn stuffy*.

"I start here tomorrow full time. Guess I'll see you around."

He lit another cigar, crossed his legs, like we hadn't just fucked right there on the sofa, and turned his head away from me.

My feelings weren't hurt, 'cause that muthafucka had to be some type of psycho. I gathered my hundreds and headed straight for the bathroom.

Chapter Four

The next night I stepped out the cab with a different attitude. The parking lot was semi-packed, and everyone who saw me caught the vapors off of my look. I'm sure some fool thought I was a superstar by the way I walked, and all eyes zoomed in on me.

I was dressed in all black Chanel, like a drive-by was on my agenda for the night. My Chanel sunglasses added to my mysterious persona; and my black Chanel oversized bag with all my necessities for the night probably puzzled people even more. I rocked so much Chanel I needed a check from their marketing department. I laughed at myself for always being so eccentric.

By the time I got to the front door, I felt like I owned the place. I'd already made it up in my mind that if I was gonna do this shit, it had to be done right. Top-notch. That was my style. Carlos taught me to never half-step with anything. *By next week, I would be Big Willy's number one money maker, and would be able to afford a decent place to lay my head.*

Once inside, I sashayed past all the hungry eye-balls and headed straight to the dressing room. Three girls stood blocking my way when I entered the back room. I started to say excuse me, but figured this would be a hostile working environment like the other two strips clubs I'd worked in the past. That's how chicks in the business rolled. Every bitch wanted to be more gangsta than the next. I decided to stand my ground early. I placed my hands on my hips and twisted my face, creating the evilest scowl possible.

"Can I help you, bitch?" some big earring-wearing heffa blared.

"Yeah…as a matter of fact, you can. I'm the new sheriff in town. As you can see, a good-looking sheriff." I turned in circles so she could check out my prize possessions. "Here to lock all your previous customers down! Bitch!" I laughed scandalously and walked directly through their little circle. The way they broke up their little clique that quickly told me they were chumps.

"Tiger, that fake bitch tried to play you," the older girl of the three announced. She looked to be in her late thirties, so I knew a few bouts with her, she'd be knocked the fuck out.

"Oh, Tiger,…" I teased. "That's all you could come up with for a stage name?" I laughed again. "It looks to me you should've named yourself Tigger. Or pussycat maybe?"

A few of the girls started laughing.

I looked at her orange and black stripped one-piece body suit and long blonde wig that swept the top of her butt cheeks, and knew instantly why she called herself a tiger. If that was all she had to offer her customers, she would be broke by next month.

At first she tried to buck back, but when the bitch walked up on me, and stood face-to-face, she knew her lil' short ass was no match. My thickness had her shook.

"Don't let this pretty face fool you," I belted.

"You think you fly?" she smacked, real ghetto-like.

"It is what it is."

I pushed my three middle fingers forcefully into her forehead, sending her body falling back slightly. I thought I saw smoke coming from the top of the bitch's head. She bolted into me like weak lightening. A fight on my first night wasn't what I expected.

31

"Oh…no you didn't!" she shouted.

"Yeah…I did!"

Her first hit didn't even faze me. She was stout, but I was solid and strong. I thought about hitting her with a left upper cut to the chin, but I didn't wanna be fired on my first day. My brother had taught me how to fight well in my younger days, so Miss Tiger was no match. I'd gone toe-to-toe with the best, even tough neighborhood enemies, who couldn't handle my punches.   I shoved her so hard, Tiger fell into a shoe rack up against the wall. As she struggled to get up, I quickly thought of my next move. I shot across the room, aiming for my purse. I grabbed it, and fumbled through it like a crackhead searching for a rock. At the feel of my razor, my wicked grin widened. Then I thought about my mace. I never left home without it.

I held my razor in the air, taunting Tiger and the other two scary bitches nearby. "This is what the fuck I'm about. If we gon' do this, let's go all the way." I pointed the razor at them all, swinging it in different positions around the room.

Suddenly, Tiger slipped away from my view, and ran for a bat in the corner of the room, which looked like it belonged in a Flintstone episode or came from someone's cave girl costume. I instantly got crazy, 'cause I wasn't gonna get beat down by no damn thick-ass bat.

My mind blacked out. I headed for Tiger at full force. First, I grabbed her dollar-store-bought wig, weave, or whatever the fuck she had going on and snatched it off with one tug. Then I punched her in the stomach forcefully, hoping I wouldn't have to put the razor to work. All I really wanted was respect. I felt her weak muscles caving in. They had no power at all. Her grip on me felt like a young battered woman trying to protect herself.

Out of the blue, loud noises were heard coming our way. They startled me. Hell, they startled us all. There was

laughter, good cheer, and mixed voices; both male and female. As they got closer, we all stopped. Fear invaded my
eyes and Tigers.

"Big Willy will throw us the hell outta here," she
quickly expressed. "He's done it before."

I just nodded my agreement. She was obviously calling
a truce.

"But this shit ain't over."

"Bitch… I know," I responded, without a care.

Two seconds later, we all turned to face two dancers
who entered the room. They both stopped to look at us
strangely as if they could sense something was going on. I
wasn't worried about the little woman, or the thick red-bone
bitch. I hesitated to see if the male voices were coming in.
However, the more I listened, the more I realized the men
were standing outside the dressing room just talking shit to
one another.

"What's up, Essence," the girls all chimed in, one after
another.

I was starting to think Essence, the thick new-comer
was some sorta superstar. She pranced past us, after staring us
all down, and began to undress right in front of everyone.
Damn, I thought. *Big, red, and beautiful.*

I followed suit, and started getting ready for the night
as well. I spent about thirty minutes watching Essence take
over the dressing room. She was quiet, yet controlling. The
more I listened to the other ladies talk, the more I felt like I'd
be able to fit in at some point. Especially when Essence
stopped to ask me if I needed anything.

"I hear you're from outta town…you a'ight?"

"Nah…I'm straight." *Now that's hot,* I thought. *She
checkin' on a bitch.*

"If you do, let me know."

"Thanks."

33

She smiled and walked out, while all the girls watched her back-side, idolizing her all along. I thought she was a hottie, but all that extra worshipping shit wasn't necessary.

I sat down in the chair and took my time preparing for my set. I needed everything to be perfect; my smell, my walk, my hair, and my freak game. I thought about how tonight, my first night on the stage, had to have negroes drooling. So I pulled out my secret ammunition; my small bottle of Crisco, baby-oil and olive oil all mixed together. Depending on the lighting, I'd know what to use.

Quickly, I pulled my shirt off, freed my boobs, and got oiled down. The moment I was done, I glued my sunflowers carefully to each breast. I laughed inside at my new hair-brain scheme. The whole flower deal had to work. By the time I'd finished, I felt like a swarm of bees would be on my ass soon. In all, there were about thirty yellow sunflowers attached to my bare skin.

When I placed the yellow silk robe around my body, I noticed Tiger watching me with envy. As soon as I bent down to grab my music from my bag, I'd already figured out a way to get her back. I grinned and walked out the room with arrogance.

The club was packed, and for the first time I got a feel for what the Magic City hype was all about. Ballers filled the room, and obviously there was some real money to be made. I watched Essence work the room like she was the shit. From lap to lap she moved, collecting a few dollars, or whispering sweet lies in some man's ear. I had to admit, a little jealously filled my heart, but I liked her style. She was just doing her, not bothering anybody. The girl who danced on the stage was boring the hell out of the guys, so I guess Essence felt she could get all of her potential money.

I checked the clock, only to see that my set was next. The dead-beat on stage was putting me to sleep. I marched over to the DJ and seductively handed him my music. "Hi, I'm Sunshine," I finally said, as he turned the music down a bit. "The new girl. The new money maker," I added.

"Damn, you got some pretty skin," he blurted out. "Not too dark…and not too light," he screeched, with some long whistle. "Damnnnn… you was cooked just right. You got Indian in yo family?" Instantly, he burst into laughter. I just didn't laugh back. I hated fast talkers.

"Enough of that shit," I said, shooting him a quick smile that disappeared as soon as I started talking. "Tonight's my first night. And I gotta make a good impression. So don't fuck it up," I told him.

"Ahh, shit now…I likes me an aggressive woman. You look like you could handle a man like me."

I just grinned, knowing I couldn't fuck with a DJ. I needed a Suga Daddy, not a muthafucka who played records for a living.

I kept feeling the DJ out, trying to see if it was the right time to slaughter Tiger. The more he looked at my left tit peeking from my robe, the time became more and more perfect.

"Look," I whispered, pulling his ear gently toward my soft lips. I whispered into his ear, making sure to sneak a few licks. The moment I finished telling him how to fuck up Tiger's music when she went on stage, I knew I had him hooked. I slipped him a fifty and licked his earlobe just to seal the deal.

"As hard as my dick is, I'll do anything for you, baby. Put your money away," he said, almost dropping his head-phones.

"Great." *I damn sho needed my fifty.*

When I heard my new friend's voice blare through the speakers, my body shook with a tad bit of nervousness. Making my way toward the back of the stage, I scanned the room looking for my targets. I knew people would wonder why I would start off my set with a silk robe, but once the music started and I dropped it, they'd get the point.

I stood like a statue toward the back of the stage, waiting for the music to start. The DJ was blowing me up, giving me all types of shout outs, like I was a true superstar. I loved it, but I needed to get busy, so the butterflies in my stomach could be put to rest.

When I heard the famous beats to Beyonce's *'Crazy In Love'* start, I put the thick soles to my bright yellow boots in motion. One by one, I strutted to the front of the stage like I was on a Vogue runway. The spectators directly in front of the stage sat up straight, showing they were finally interested in the entertainment. I stopped center stage and bent all the way down to grab both my ankles. My robe flew open, revealing that I was almost ass-naked, only slightly covered by flowers.

"Fellas, get yo money ready for Miss Sunshine," the DJ announced.

Yells and claps sounded from all around the room. I even saw Big Willy's fat-ass back by the bar clapping too. I guess he liked the new stage name I had chosen, or maybe it was the outfit.

Without further delay, I dropped my robe, swung it in the air and worked my body slowly to the upbeat music. Within minutes, my skin produced a light sweat, causing my honey colored skin to glow even more. The crowd was going crazy, and the bills were now waving in the air. I needed to hold out, making sure the right amount of money flowed in. My goal was to capture it all in the crack of my ass. So, I danced around for the next couple of minutes, sending the men into a frenzy.

Once I made it to the edge of the stage, I was ready for the famous booty crunch, and figured it was time to collect my cash. I scooted on all fours backwards to the edge, flashing my ass in the faces of the three men front and center. Before I knew it, there was like a stampede of donors headed to the stage. From the corner of my eye, I could see one of the club's bodyguards headed that way too, so I continued my outlandish dance. I grinded and shook my ass preparing to get my, uh…oh…uh…oh, booty thing going.

Just about the same time that I shook my ass like it was going into convulsions, I felt the cold feeling of dollar bills sliding into the crack of my ass. I squeezed my cheeks tightly, embedding the bills in place and shook even more.

"What the fuck we got going on here?" the DJ shouted. "Sunshine got 'em going crazy! Know that she likes any kind of bill that spends, but she's good friends with Benjamin Franklin. George Washington don't fuck too good," he joked.

He turned the music up even louder, and blended in some song I'd never heard of. It was obviously an ATL favorite, 'cause the place went wild. I had so much money coming they started sticking it in my boots.

When my set ended, I was officially a Magic City superstar by round of applause. They clapped and cheered as I walked off stage, and lame-ass Tiger walked on. She shot me an evil look, and I responded with my fabulous walk. I winked over at the DJ before disappearing, confirming our little agreement.

Damn, I love how I always got a trick up my sleeve, I thought. A huge smile spread across my face and I immediately started laughing when DJ Funk's song '*There's Some Hoe's in This House*' started playing. It was the perfect choice.

Chapter Five

The next morning I woke up to a terrible feeling. A feeling that damn sho never conquered me before. Nor, did I wish on my worst enemy. I raised my aching body from the hotel bed and clutched my stomach tightly. The dreadful pains were beating me up inside like I'd stolen something from my wound, and he/she or it was paying my ass back. I couldn't pin point if it was my pelvic area, my organs, or what, but it was kicking my ass.

My thoughts drifted back to the greasy fried chicken wings with extra mumbo sauce I'd eaten the night before. "That couldn't be it," I said to myself.

Slowly, I inched my way to the bathroom, taking step by step. For some reason my strides were slow, sluggish, and extra lazy-like. Me being physically drained couldn't be explained. I thought deeply about what could be happening. I thought back to how I ended up hanging out with Stacy from here at the hotel last night after the club closed. She was turning out to be real cool, and sexy too. So when she challenged me to a drinking contest at some run-down bar, I thought nothing of it. I drunk her little dark-skinned ass under the table.

"Hennessy, nah…that wouldn't have me feeling like this," I reasoned with myself.

Just as I got near the bathroom door, a strong jilt shot through my gut and knocked me off balance. My right hand latched onto the frame of the door to help keep me steady. I breathed deeply and caught my breath, just long enough to step onto the cold, tiled floor. Once inside, I flicked on the lights, and quickly squatted to piss.

Instantly, I flinched and screamed out loud! A burning sensation caused me to tighten up down below. My piss burned like hell, so I struggled to keep the rest from coming out.

Suddenly, my eyes focused down below. From the lining in my panties to the toilet bowl, I looked back and forth. Blood? I wondered, why. This was scary!

Between the sudden spotting and the painful aching, it all had me shook. I snatched a big wad of tissue from the roll and blotted my pussy fretfully. A light colored spot of blood confirmed once again that something was up.

Tears flooded my face about the same time the phone started ringing. At first I ignored it, thinking no one knew my whereabouts. Then my mind started fuckin' with me. Maybe it was Carlos. Maybe he'd come to his senses, and was looking for me? I moved as fast as my body would allow, headed across the room to the phone. The moment I answered, a sharp stabbing pain caught me, and had my voice sounding crazy.

"Hel…lo…" I barely mumbled.

"See, I knew you couldn't handle me. That Hen-Dog got you fucked up, ain't it?"

Both my hormones and emotions were going wild. Just hearing Stacy's voice made me break out into a hysterical sob. I acted as if I'd known her all my life. "Something's wrong, Stacy. I can feel it."

"Girl, calm down. What's wrong?"

"It hurt soooooo bad," I cried out in pain.

"What is it?"

"Are you here at work, or at home?" I moaned, feeling a bit faint.

All of a sudden I started to only hear muffled echoing

sounds. Stacy was talking, but I couldn't make it out. The sounds continued, but I was done. Before I knew it, the phone dropped from my hand, and my body fell to the floor.

***

"Girl, you all fucked up," Stacy blared into my face.

The moment I opened my eyes, I looked around the room, wondering why the crisp, white hospital room ended up being my new chill spot. "What happened to me?"

Stacy could tell by my stare that I wanted answers. But, I was so afraid. Afraid of the answer. Afraid of the damn near 300 pound nurse coming my way. Afraid of everybody.

"They wouldn't tell me," Stacy answered, with pity in her eyes. "They talking some bullshit 'bout I gotta be family to know your private info."

A lump formed in my throat. "Must be serious, huh?"

"I'm just trying to look out for you, that's all." Stacy directed her eyes to the fat-ass nurse, who was now calling my doctor since my eyes were open. It was obvious the nurse had pissed her off. "I'm glad you a'ight, girl. You scared the shit outta me."

The minute Stacy moved closer to my bed and grabbed my hand, I thought about how much she could be trusted. I mean... I'd only known her for a few days. But, we shared enough family secrets last night, which would now make her an honorary family member, especially since I never talked to my own.

Stacy revealed that she was twenty-six, so she wasn't too far behind me. She also told me that she had family members who were just like my dysfunctional-ass family. On the real, it made me smile inside. She really did seem like family. Oddly, Stacy even reminded me of my nosey cousin, Vicki.

The only difference showed in their style of dress. Stacy wasn't big on trendy clothing. Most times, she rocked slip on shoes, form-fitting jeans to show off her shape, and a pair of worn down flip flops. She was just a lot shorter Vicki, with a big-man attitude.

It seemed like the more we talked, the closer we became, and the more my lust for her decreased. She seemed to be a good friend to have around.

Just then, Stacy caught me off guard. She gripped my hands tighter as I tried to pull back. I had always been self-conscious about my hands, and today they really needed an emergency manicure. "Stop pulling away from me!" she shouted.

"My hands just feel rough, that's all," I replied.

"Well shit, I'll grab you some lotion out your purse if that's the case."

I hesitated, not really wanting her all up in my personal shit, but it was too late.

"Why are you a grown-ass woman still carrying a razor blade," she joked. "You's a razor hoe."

Our laughter was cut short when a tall, striking gentleman walked in wearing a white lab coat.

"Ms Martinez, I'm Doctor Wallace. I'm gonna need to speak to you alone. I'm gonna have to ask your friend to leave the room."

He looked at Stacy. Stacy looked at me. I looked toward the wall.

"Tell 'em, Chanel. Tell 'em I'm fam."

"It's okay, Stacy. I don't wanna cause no confusion. You know they like to say us black folk cause trouble wherever we go." I snickered, showing the doctor and everybody that I was feeling better. "Just wait outside."

"Oooookayyyyyy. If you say so. But you really need somebody in here with you. They might be trying to steal your damn kidneys or some shit."

I laughed.

"I'm fo real. I seen that shit in a movie once." Stacy brushed past the doctor and moved toward the door with a smirk on her face. Sassy should've been her middle name. *Love it*, I thought.

"Stacy, do me a favor?" I yelled out.

"Sure. What is it?" She stood by the door, pressing her short hair into place.

"Call Big Willy at my job and tell 'em I'm in the hospital. Let him know I'll be out by tomorrow."

"Who said?" the doctor quickly asked.

"Damn, girl, what, you got AIDS or some shit."

I just shot her *a 'no you didn't look'*. "Just call 411 to get the number."

"A'ight. I'm out."

When the door shut, my heart rate sped and the machine went wild. Dr. Wallace remained calm. He pressed a few buttons on the machine and checked the flow of my IV. My breathing intensified waiting to hear what he had to say.

"Why don't you start?" the doctor suggested.

"Where?"

"Whatever you think I should know."

"Well, all I remember is being in my hotel room and…"

"Nooooo." He shook his head with disappointment. " Not that."

"What?" My eyebrows creased. He could tell I was confused.

"Is there something you want to tell me? Or let me rephrase. What do you think I need to know?"

When Doctor Wallace gave me that look, the look a scolding parent would give, I knew what he was talking about. But, I didn't want to discuss it at the moment. I wasn't feeling too good all of a sudden. So I just lowered my head, hoping he'd go away.

"It's a must that we discuss it. I've got to know your history. All of it," he drilled.

I knew it was time to use my drama skills. I held my head low and threw it into the palms of my hands. My cries were loud. Louder than he'd obviously heard in a while. He showed a funny-looking expression, and decided to pull up a chair. That was my cue that I'd been defeated. He wasn't going anywhere.

"Well, Ms. Martinez, we'll have to wait 'til you calm down, won't we?"

"I cried even more, hoping the day would just end.

Chapter Six

Eavesdropping outside Big Willy's door made me smile. I'd just finished my set, and heard him bragging about how glad he was that I was back. My five day absence must've made him realize my worth. The regulars had only seen my big-boned ass perform twice before my hospital bout, but was feenin' for a lil' sunshine. I thought, *show me the money, nigga.*

Even Essence's big ass was jockin' me when I came off stage. Niggas was clapping like they hadn't seen nobody work it like that in years. From the sounds of things, I was gonna have to ask Big Willy for a raise real soon. I laughed at how I thought about things. I damn sho need some extra cash.

Stacy showed she was down for a sistah when she let me crash at her crib last night after I got released. That $49.00 shit at the hotel was killing me. I just couldn't afford it anymore. So, the next best thing was sleeping on the floor at Stacy's one bedroom efficiency. It was low budget but clean. I appreciated it though, even though it was hard keeping my feelings in the right place when it came to Stacy. Especially the way she would lotion those muscular ass legs after coming in from the gym.

I heard Big Willy coming my way, so I took my mind off Stacy and my feet got to moving. As soon as I passed the pay phone, it reminded me that I needed to call my mother. Money was a big issue. Plus, I had questions that only she could answer about my blood type. I wanted to call from Stacy's, but figured keeping her out my business would keep our friendship longer.

I lifted the receiver, and instantly got nervous. The music in the background was a little noisy, but helped to keep my mind off what was about to happen. I hadn't talked to her in over two months, and hoped like hell she would take my collect call. Just as the operator asked me my name, Essence came by and slapped me on my ass while talking on level ten.

"Hey, your mute lover just came in. He reserved the VIP section all to himself, and he asking for you, baby girl. Matter of fact, he's been here every day for the last five days, looking for your sweet ass. Pussy must be good." She laughed loudly, and popped her gum real ghetto-like.

My eyes swiveled around. I wanted to ask more questions about Mr. Mute, who wouldn't tell me his name when we fucked the same day I was hired, but the operator kept asking me for my name.

"Finally," I said, "Chanel."

I waited patiently while she connected the call. When my mother answered, my emotions flared. I don't know why, but the sound of her voice made me drop a tear. "Ma!" I yelled out, but she couldn't hear me, only the operator.

"Collect call from Chanel," the operator said.

"Who?" I could hear my mother saying. I wanted to yell louder. But I knew she couldn't hear me. "Who?" she repeated several times. Then finally said the word that crushed my heart. "I'm sorry, I don't know any Chanels." Then hung up.

My heart dropped to my shoe. But I had to snap back, 'cause Essence was back in my face again.

"Gurl, what you looking all crazy for?" She grabbed me by the hand firmly. Strangely, we connected. Her hands were just as large as mine, but she took control. "Come with me."

"Where we going? I gotta gotta…make…make another call," I stuttered.

"Uhhh…huh. Later. Right now, you gotta make this money. You see this here." She stopped in the middle of the floor and flashed a sweaty fifty dollar bill she pulled from her bra. "That high roller over there gave it to me."

She pointed to one of the VIP sections. The same VIP section where I freaked my non-talking lover last week.

"He gave me fifty in advance just to bring your ass to him. He sweet on you. Now go get that money and stop playin'." She slapped me on my ass again.

My conscious wanted to tell Essence that was the last time she would get a pass for slapping me on my ass. But she didn't appear to be gay, so I figured no harm. And even though I lusted after women every now and then, I didn't consider myself gay. Besides, Essence was fine, but wasn't my type. Too tall. Too big. Too dominate. Imagine our two big asses bumping bodies. I laughed at the thought.

"Well, let me give my mute man what he's asking for," I finally said to Essence.

"Do that. He a high profile dude. So if he requesting you like that, it'll up your worth around here."

"High profile? Who is he?"

"I'll tell you later." She pushed me along.

When I walked up the steps to VIP, my customer was smoking his cigar, and the same scent from before invaded my nose. I eyed him intently, while I put my seductive walk in full throttle. My stride was lethal, and could snag the best of the best. I just wondered who my mystery man really was, and why he was on me so hard. Maybe the mayor of some small town? Or maybe somebody in the music business? Whoever he was, he was about to get done right. I needed to put the mojoe on his ass, 'cause I needed money bad, and wanted him salivating at the mouth for more. This time, the goal was nine hundred.

I thought about the fact that my court date for my credit card fraud charge back in Detroit was coming up in a few weeks, and I needed money to pay a lawyer fast. Jail was no place for me. Been there done that.

With that said, I walked right up to my customer and yanked him by his purple country looking tie. Whoever he was, he damn sho couldn't dress. His old fashioned pinstriped suit, which also had a high waist looked like it belonged on the pimp from the movie, '*I'm Gonna Get You Sucka*'. I eyed him, momentarily checking out his multi-colored Stacy Adams shoes, and then grabbed his hand.

I led him to the plush red velour couch that sat in the middle of the sectioned off VIP area. Again, he sat staring at me from head to toe, but didn't muster a word. His eyes did all the talking, and they pierced right through me.

"So, Mr…what's your name again?" I asked, but knew he had never told me his name. "You been missing this pussy I heard. Came back for more, huh?" I shrugged my shoulders with more confidence than was needed.

Mr. Mute nodded and removed the cigar from his lips and sat his Courvoisier on the glass end table. I decided to make my move. *Might as well get this party started*, I thought. The quicker it's started, the faster it will be over, and the quicker I got paid.

I slid out of my new black robe, and stood snobbishly in front of him wedged between his legs. Wearing a black leather bustier and matching thong, I knew I was the shit. My four-inch stilettos caused my ass to sit high in the air. As I was slowly unfastening the corset of the bustier, he reached up and forcefully ripped it open. Exposing my full D cup breast, my nipples hardened immediately from the cool draft.

"Damn, baby, I like it rough, but I'm gonna have to add that to your bill." I spoke with attitude and rolled my eyes daringly.

Still he said nothing. Instead, he pulled me close so that he could feast on my breast. He was rougher than before, but it was a good rough. His mysterious ways were turning me on so much. He grabbed each breast and sucked hard, just like a hungry child anxious to be nursed by his mother. His lips smacked as his tongue slowly circled each nipple causing goose bumps to rise all over my body. My knees felt weak, and I used his body as a crutch to keep from falling.

Just when I was really getting into the groove of things, Mr. Mute spoke surprisingly. "Bend over the couch."

His words were demanding and had not one ounce of sincerity. But, for some reason, it was a turn on. So, I obeyed his wishes, while he unloosened his tie and unzipped his pants.

"So, Mr. Mystery, you wanna hit this doggy style, huh?"

I asked him that just to spark up some fire, 'cause on the real, I despised the doggy style position, but I pretended to go along with it anyway. Men hate it when they hear the no word. I clutched his dick and turned to face him.

"I got something better than hitting it from the back. You wanna feel it?" I asked seductively.

He said absolutely nothing.

"Come get this pussy," I whispered, and licked my lips seductively.

Within minutes the silent stranger held my ass cheeks apart and let the head of his dick just touch the opening, never entering. I wasn't used to my customers teasing me or trying to satisfy me, but I was enjoying this moment. His manhood needed no guidance from his hand, 'cause his position was perfectly lined up with my entrance. He watched as his shaft disappeared into my deepness and mounds of cream appeared on his dark meat.

"Ahh, damn!" the muted man finally moaned in ecstasy, while taking deep breaths.

"Give me that dick, baby!"

My pussy smacked with wetness. I pushed forcefully onto his erection, and my well-lubricated pussy took in all of him, causing him to moan and clinch his eyes tightly.

Prince's '*Darling Nikki*' played loudly in the club for the stripper who was presently on the stage. We rocked in unison to the beat of the music, while pleasing each other. Mr. Mute released my ass cheeks, banging against me and his balls slapping my clit. I contracted my vaginal walls to grab my client's dick tightly and he gasped loudly.

"Oh, oh, yeah. Hell…yeah! Wooorrrkkk it. You gonna make me bust."

I almost lost my train of thought. The psycho actually said more than two words. Damn near a complete sentence. Sweat fell from his forehead and landed on my belly.

Surprisingly, I was near an orgasm. That shit didn't happen often when fucking a client. Most times, I worked the fake-me-out game. But, it is what it is, so I just leaned my head back and enjoyed the ride for a change.

Just then my silent customer leaned forward, and with both hands, grabbed a hold of my shoulders, pulling me toward him with every push he gave me. The pace picked up double time; his manhood was deep inside me and hitting every wall. I could feel my explosion nearing, so I fucked him back intensely. Mr. Mute grinded in and out, round and round.

"Ohh, this pussy is so good," the nameless man said between breaths.

"Yeah, baby, fuck me. Make me cum all over that dick," I replied, looking him dead in the face.

Just as I was reaching my climax, I felt his cum on the rise. I could feel his dick pulsating inside me. His strokes were deep, fast and hard. I knew he would explode at any moment.

Almost out of breath, he pulled his short thick dick from my pussy and nutted all over my skin. In shock, my mouth fell open. Not sure why he pulled out, I just kept my mind on my money. He collapsed for a brief second between my tits, trying to catch his breath. Instinct caused my body to lean back a bit, giving him an escape to ease up from the couch. No time for sentiments, this was business. My pussy juices were still dripping on the red velour couch beneath me. By the time I turned around and held my hand out for my loot, Mr. Mute had zipped his pants and was rushing away.

"Wait!" I yelled, trying to fix my bustier. "I know this nigga not trying to play me," I said.

I got ready for war. Fighting my six foot three pussy thief would be a task, probably more of an embarrassment. But he was about to get it. Fuckin with my loot was a no no.

By the time I slipped my heels back on, my eyes scanned the small table to my left where several bills caught my attention. I stopped in my tracks, ran over and scurried through the money. Seven hundred dollar bills and two fifties sat waiting just for me. I turned to thank him, but he had completely disappeared. I just smiled. A big smile.

***

The moment my body hit the outside air, I noticed my strut was different. I was sho nuff changing. Although my feet followed Essence to her truck, my mind got side-tracked by the whistles coming from behind.

"Yo, yo, Miss Lady, you did your thing in there," a fan yelled from behind.

"Wit yo sexy ass!" another bystander hollered.

I just smiled and hopped up in the truck. The comments had the complete opposite effect on Essence. She rolled her eyes and gritted her teeth like a beat down was headed their way.

"I gotta stop by Starbucks and get me a muthafuckin Latte before we head to your crib," Essence revealed to me.

I was tired but just nodded. There was no need in complaining when I didn't have another ride. I leaned back and sat quietly on the short ride around the corner. For some strange reason, I could feel Essence looking at me, but she didn't say anything. So, I didn't either. When she whipped the Escalade into the parking lot of the twenty-four hour Starbucks, I told her to leave the keys, 'cause I planned on chilling 'til she came back.

"Bitch, let's go," she ordered, without even looking my way.

"I'm staying."

"No…you not. This my whip."

I reared up in my seat, ready to serve the bitch, until she justified herself.

"Look, just come with me. Besides, I wanna turn you on to something."

Her tone lightened, and my tired body eased out the truck. We walked inside. with Essence comfortably pressing her hand on my shoulder for guidance.

As soon as we hit the door, a striking deep golden-toned man caught my attention as he reached for his change at the register. His full head of dreads were noticeable from the door. His frame, tall and well-built had me shook. When we walked past each other, he sipped his coffee and gave me a quick seductive glance. I felt like a goof when I bumped into the person in front of me trying to follow his stare.

"Turn the fuck around. And don't be so desperate," Essence taunted, then rolled her eyes at me.

"It's not being desperate. He was fineeee…and he was watching me like crazy. Shit, my every movement, bitch. Stop hatin'."

Essence didn't respond. She shooed me off with a

wave of the hand and ordered drinks for us. When she handed me my coffee on the way out the door, I was expecting it to taste like something I'd never tasted before. It damn sho didn't.

"What the hell is this? This is the special drink you wanted to turn me on to?"

"Yeah. It's a Cinnamon Latte. Isn't it good?"

"Next time, save your money," I said, headed to the truck, and tossing my cup into the trash at the same time.

"Oh, so you gon' waste my damn money? Bitch, do you know that shit cost $4.00?"

"Your ass shoulda' left me in the truck where I wanted to stay in the first place."

"Well then, pretty lady, I wouldn't have seen your beautiful smile today," a voice said from behind.

I turned at the sound of the deep baritone, island-sounding voice. His smile made me knot up inside. Essence hopped in the truck and slammed the door, just as my new friend introduced himself.

"Samuel," he said, extending his hand.

"Chanel," my shaky voice uttered. I knew I had a high pitched tone on a normal day, but his presence made me nervous and my voice extra squeaky. I couldn't believe I was getting all choked up. He spoke in perfect English dialect, but I could tell he was from some type of Jamaican or island descent.

"You from around here, beautiful?" he asked.

"Ahh...sort of."

"What kinda answer is that?"

I smiled. He smiled back even wider. He looked over at Essence and gave a funny mocking look.

"Looks like your girl is in a hurry. You wanna stay and have a cup of coffee so we can chit chat. I'll make sure you get home safe."

"Nah…maybe another day."

"Okay, well can I at least have a number where I can reach you."

I couldn't think fast enough, so I grabbed a pen from my purse and scribbled Stacy's number down as fast as I could. "Call me," I said, backing up toward the door.

I wanted to keep the conversation brief, 'cause Essence looked like she wanted to pull off and leave me. Besides, his firm body was chiseled and was making me wet right there in the damn parking lot.

"I will. Trust me." He just kept nodding and eyeing me down from head to toe.

Damn his voice sounded good to me. The moment I stepped into the truck, Essence pulled off going fifty out the parking lot. Even though the truck was peeling out the lot on two wheels, I still managed to sneak Samuel a girlish wave. He waved back and held his hand toward his ear mouthing the words, *I'll call you*. It didn't hurt that he'd pointed his alarm key toward a brand spankin new black Bentley Continental GT. The $150,000 coupe instantly made my panties moist.

I grinned a long grin, until Essence destroyed my little happy moment. "You so damn gullible. Any nigga with a three dollar smile and a dick print can snag you. Be selective, bitch."

"Why the fuck are you so worried about what I do? Or for that matter, who I do?"

"I'm just saying, this guy don't seem right. It's something about him. I can spot muthafuckas with a bad vibe from anywhere. Besides you already got a sneaky ass corrupt pastor on your tip. Deal with that for now. At least you getting paid."

I turned to look at Essence. My jaw was still lowered nearing my chin. "What?" I questioned.

"That's right. Your mystery man at the club is a pastor.

He's corrupt as hell, but he sweet on you."

"Right here," was all I could say as we pulled onto Stacy's block. Her building was right in front of me, but I was still in shock, and couldn't open the door just yet. I heard Essence unlock the door from her side, but I just sat.

"Damn, this is a dump," she commented.

I heard her voice, but kept thinking 'bout the Pastor and Samuel.

"Get the fuck out!" Essence shouted. "I'll check you later. Call me if you need a ride somewhere."

I eased out the car, but my mind remained stuck on fluster mode.

Chapter Seven

Days went by with no word from Samuel. Unfortunately for me, his scent still lingered on my mind. For some reason, my hormones were acting up again, and I grudgingly wanted to punch Stacy's wall since he hadn't called. Just the remembrance of his fine features and chiseled body had me wanting to finger myself. Just the thought of his peculiar accent sent chills through my spine. Then, within seconds anger filled my spirit. I thought about punching myself in the forehead for not going home with him the first night we met.

I was starting to think my age was catching up with me with all my crazy mood swings. Jay-Z said thirty was the new twenty, but damn, he should've been more specific about my twenty-seven year old ass. My old pussy had been through the wringer more than a few times. Possibly a few thousand. And my mind was now paying the price.

Maybe the thought of Friday coming up had me jilted. I had promised Stacy that I was moving by Friday, so she could have her space back. But money was looking a little low. I'd saved about $2,000.00, but needed $3,500.00 for my new apartment. Since I didn't have any credit, the woman at the leasing office told me I would have to put down a security deposit of two months rent. It amazed me how people always talked about how Atlanta housing was so reasonable. I hadn't come across a plush apartment that I called reasonable yet.

When Stacy hung up her cell phone, it was the perfect opportunity to ask if I could stay an extra week. She walked past me shuffling clothes around the small space.

"Uh…Stacy. I gotta holla at you about something."

"Nope. I'm broke." She smiled. "That is what you want, right?" She looked back at me, waiting for an answer.

"No. I…"

The phone rang, causing me to stop mid-sentence and leap across the couch. I prayed it would be Samuel.

"Hello."

I stood dumbfounded. The voice on the other line was deep, yet so familiar. Clearly, it wasn't my new dream man. "How'd you get this number?" I asked, while looking at Stacy. I didn't really want her to hear the conversation. The last time I'd spoken to my brother it was a heated exchange of words.

"You called me from this number earlier, didn't you?"

I covered the phone with my hand and moved to the side. Now wasn't a good time to talk. "Look, I did call you earlier. I needed a favor, but I'm straight now. I'll call you a little later." I glanced over to see if Stacy had started to pay more attention to my weird conversation.

"You haven't called me in over a year and a half, why now?"

"I'm having some issues, that's all."

"Why not call Daddy?"

"That was low, Jerell." He knew damn well my history with our father. It was an issue only the Good Lord would be able to handle. "Look, Jerell. I'm not looking for an argument. Just tell Mama I said hello."

I hung up fast before I'd have to answer some shit that I just didn't want to address. No sooner than I escaped one strange altercation, Stacy was right in my grill questioning me.

"Who was that?"

"Uhh… my…brother."

"Girl, I didn't know you had a brother. You never said

nothing. Why you always so damn secretive?"

"Well, think about it. You haven't known me that long. Now have you?"

"I guess you're right. I always wanted a brother," she revealed, while folding the remaining clothes thrown over the chair.

Her comment made me think of Jerell. We had once been so close growing up. Inseparable, I remember my mother saying. He was the more outgoing one, while I was more into show-boating. Flaunting nice cars, clothes and jewelry was my thing. But he never gave up on me. He was considered the more likely to succeed between the two of us, yet he coached me and pulled me up on his coat tail until I left home rebelliously. He told me to always maintain my self-esteem no matter what the circumstances were ahead of me, and I've never forgotten those words. I laughed at the fact that he was the one who even taught me how to box. *Talk about well rounded. I guess that's why I can fuck a muthafucka up when necessary.*

"Chanel!" you hear me Stacy yelled. She'd obviously been calling me for a minute, while in my trance.

Then a sudden knock at the door side-tracked us both.

"Who is it?" Stacy shouted. The peep hole had been cracked for weeks and still hadn't been fixed. So Stacy just stood waiting for a response. "Who the fuck is it?" she asked again.

Stacy turned and looked at me strangely.

"What?" I questioned. My shoulders shrugged.

"Sounds like they asking for you. Who the fuck you got coming to my place?"

I just looked at Stacy and moved in front of her, closer to the door. "Who is it?"

When I heard Essence's voice, I opened the door quickly. "Is everything alright?"

She strutted in with a wicked smile. "I guess so, if you call living in a dump alright."

Stacy's dark skin frowned. Her look of disapproval displayed as they locked eyes.

Essence crossed her arms and twitched her lips. "Truth hurts don't it."

"Chanel, you gotta take your rude-ass company outside. Some people don't know to show respect when you're in someone's house."

"Respect, huh? You gotta be kidding me." Essence rolled her eyes as hard as she possibly could.

Stacy whipped her neck around. She looked at me to help her out, all awhile smoke steamed from her nose.

"Essence, let's talk outside," I suggested.

"For what? I came to help you escape this rat hole. When I dropped you off the other night, I couldn't even sleep. Consider me your savior." She laughed. "I say get your shit and come camp out at my place until your apartment comes through. I got a two bedroom with plenty of space."

"Until she decides, you gotta go. Get the fuck out!" Stacy pointed her un-manicured finger with vengeance.

Her sudden outburst shocked the hell outta me. I walked with hesitance and opened the door for Essence, but she didn't move. Even though Stacy stood three footsteps from her face, her frozen state had my adrenaline pumping. I was grateful for how Stacy, a perfect stranger, had come to my rescue, but Essence's offer sounded sweet. *My own room until I could get myself together*. Guilt built up inside.

"Look, Essence, I'll think about it. Let's just talk at the club this evening."

"Hell no. I went against my gut the other night. Let's go." She threw her hands up to the side of her hips. "I know you just need a push."

"Oh...you want a fucking push!" Stacy shouted. She

lunged toward Essence with her finger extended, and headed straight for her face.

Essence never flinched. But I decided to grab Stacy anyway, just to diffuse any body punches from going down. Damn, having two people who just wanted to help me go to blows wasn't cool. I had to do something. Plus I was scared. Scared to hurt Stacy's feelings. Scared to lose another friend. Too many losses in life already. From my mother, to my entire family, to Carlos.

Most importantly, I was scared to tell Essence no. Why, I didn't know, 'cause if I had to throw my hands up and fight Essence, I would. If that didn't work, I'd be willing to get down and dirty. But I really thought the move would be best for me. In a crazy sort of way, Essence reminded me of a dude. She was strong willed and slightly controlling. I let it go for now, 'cause I knew she meant well.

"Go on, Chanel. I know you wanna go. I see it in your eyes," Stacy said to me.

"No. I don't...really."

"Yeah, you do. It's cool. You were gonna leave here on Friday anyway." Even though her words seemed sincere, her face was still red with anger.

Within minutes, I made my decision. Stacy was my girl, but her spot was too tight. She needed her space and I needed mine. Essence's spot seemed to fit the bill until I could get my paper straight.

"Bet, I'm going," I finally said.

Stacy folded her arms. "No problem. Keep in touch."

She turned to walk away, as my body stood stiff watching her every move. She headed directly into the bathroom, shut the door, and turned the shower water on. I was hurt. Stacy didn't even help me pack up, or see me to the door.

The first thing I grabbed were my ole faithful pills. I

popped the top and took two, trying to make up for the one I missed yesterday. It was clear the pills were important, 'cause I downed them both with no chaser. Once I located all my meds, it took me about another twenty minutes to gather up the rest of my shit, before I headed down the steps.

By the time I got outside, Essence had pulled her Escalade to the front of the building and had Beyonce's '*Upgrade U*' blasting. Funny as it sounded, it was almost as if she thought the song applied to our situation. I opened the back door, looking like a bag lady with my duffel bags and boxes of boots.

"What's all that shit?"

"My clothes, and of course my boots."

"Ummh. You shoulda left all that shit. We 'bout to make money, baby. We buying all new shit."

"Hell no, I wasn't gonna leave my boots."

"Here, this is for you," Essence said, handing the sleek item my way.

"What?"

"Yeah, you heard me. For you."

I looked at the cell phone carefully. "Why in the hell are you giving me a phone?"

"Girl, consider it a gift. I'll let you know when your bill is due. But every human being over the age of eight has a cell phone."

We laughed like two good friends. Then I studied the sleek silver colored phone and smiled. "Now that's hot."

"Nah... you hot."

Essence's comment caught me off guard. I wasn't sure what she meant, but she wasn't my type. Besides, my lust for women had been wiped away for the week. I was only interested in Samuel for now. Damn, being strictly dickly might prove to be a struggle.

Chapter Eight

Only a week had passed, just enough time to get my life on a better track. Emotionally, I'd seemed to calm down and chill more than before. Money was flowing, and like I'd predicted, I was the queen of Magic City.

My set had just ended, so I slowly pranced off the stage like a superstar and made my way toward the back. To my surprise, I walked dead smack into a showdown. Essence had her hands clutched around the skinny neck of the newest addition to the dance team.

"Now remember what the fuck I said," she taunted.

Tiger had her ashy looking arms folded, and her lips poked out like she was the damn referee. I was expecting a dramatic showdown, but when she turned to see me standing in place, Essence let go of her grip. Tiger shot me a nasty look like I'd ruined everything.

"What the fuck you looking at?" I was ready to blast her again. I never liked that bitch from day one. There was just something about her. I couldn't pin point it.

Saved by the bell, one of the bouncers shouted from outside the door, "Somebody needs to see you, Sunshine."

My eyes popped open wide. I prayed it was my preacher friend. I hadn't seen him in over a week, and my pockets needed to be nursed. I pushed my boobs up high in my tight red corset shirt and strutted outside the door, giving all the girls in the back my ass to kiss.

When I hit the corner, I stopped momentarily when I saw her. This was a big surprise. Why would she be here at my job? "Stacy," I questioned with a smile. "What are you doing here?"

"Just came by to check you out, Ms. Sunshine," Stacy joked. "I caught you at the end of your routine. You're really good. Probably got the men around here drooling, huh?"

"Well, I hate to toot my own horn, but…a bitch is working these niggas up in here!"

Stacy laughed then looked around like the atmosphere was foreign to her. "It took a little bit of convincing before the bouncer would even go back and get you. He acted like I'm a stalker or some shit."

"Yeah, security has to be tight, 'cause some of the men that come up in here are crazy as hell," I chuckled. "So, this is a pleasant surprise. Here take a seat." I pulled her chair out like a hostess at a restaurant. She just looked at me strangely. "What did I do to deserve such royal treatment?" I asked.

"I guess I just miss you, that's all."

"Yeah, let's have a girl's day out next week. You know, get our hair done. Well, get my hair done, 'cause I see you still washing and gelling your hair down flat to your scalp." I shook my head and laughed at my low maintenance friend. "At least you got a good enough grade to do that shit with short hair. A broad like me gots to keep me a fresh weave."

I swung my hair from side to side, showing my conceited personality. We both laughed for a quick second, then Stacy's facial expression changed. The joyful energy turned a nasty sour.

"I really wanted to bring this envelope by. I assumed you used my address when you went to the hospital. I guess this was the doctor's initial way of getting in touch with you."

I grabbed the envelope, wondering if she'd read my mail. I tried to play it cool, knowing what the circumstances were inside. My poker face was etched on. My concern was whether Stacy was buying it.

Stacy looked at me like she'd known me her whole life. I wanted to give her dry lips a splash of lip gloss.

"Chanel, we girls, right?"

"You know it, gurl." I flashed my fake-me-out smile and gave her a high five.

"Then level with me. I'm concerned about you. I guess when you didn't respond after the doctor sent this letter, they tried calling you at my house."

My face collapsed right there at the table. I couldn't fake it anymore.

"I guess that was the only number you'd given them. You hear me, Chanel? You hear me?" she repeated.

"Yeah, I hear you. No big deal, I'll call 'em."

"Chanel, doctors don't just call wanting to know if you got the mail they sent out! Doctors don't normally do that, understand? You hear me! I'm no fool, Chanel."

I kept the envelope tight in my hands, rotating from one hand to the other, never once giving Stacy a chance to look me in the eye.

"Look, I gotta get back to work."

"Sure," she responded, with a smirk. "When you're ready to be straight with me, I'm ready to listen. See ya around."

When Stacy got up, I noticed Big Willy trying to get my attention from the far left corner. I'm sure he wanted to know the name of my tight-bodied friend, and if she needed a job. Her juicy round ass was perfect for the club. But Stacy was too feisty, and not lady-like at all. She was built to be in a controlling position, more like a correctional institution. Suddenly, she stopped and turned.

"I almost forgot. Somebody named Samuel called you too. Here's the number."

I rushed her like a linebacker and grabbed the paper from her hand. I hugged her tightly. "Thanks girl. This is the guy I told you about. I'll holla soon. I promise." I shot her a smile. She shot me one right back.

As soon as she walked away, I rushed into the bathroom with the good news in my right hand... *Samuel's number of course.* And the bad news in my left... *the doctor's assessment.* Ripping the seal on the envelope was easy. It had no real stickiness to it anymore, which had me convinced Stacy had read my damn mail. *That shit is a federal offense*, I thought.

The moment the letter was completely unfolded, my eyes darted to the center of the page. The doctor had scribbled a handwritten note across the block that read special notes. I held the palm of my right hand close to my heart. What the fuck? I never knew this would be that difficult.

A terrible sickness rose up in the pit of my stomach. Almost made me wanna vomit. Holding on to my stomach tightly, sweat began to pour. I always knew there was a strong possibility that my medical condition would come back to haunt me. But damn, abnormalities in my blood? And now all these medical complications.

All kinds of thoughts entered my mind. For a moment, I decided to throw punches at myself, while I cried like a baby. It didn't matter if anyone walked in. My life was going downhill. I had serious issues that needed to be dealt with. My body twirled inside the little stall, wondering what my next move would be. I thought about calling my mother again.

"Damn, damn, damn," I repeated to myself.

If I ever needed support, I needed it now. The thought of my mother back at home in D-Town reminded me that I had to go home in three weeks for my court date. The credit card fraud shit for once in my life got me all twisted.

The letter was important...real important. So I knew a call to the doctor was necessary. But my first move was to call Samuel. I wiped what was left of my tears, and darted from the bathroom. I needed some TLC, and Samuel was just the man to give it to me.

*****

Not even six hours went by before Samuel was on his way to get me. I was in the mirror getting all dolled up for my soon-to-be-man. I'd gone over to Monica's, my new hair-dresser in town, and got my weave washed and tightened. Thank God, Essence wasn't home, 'cause she woulda flipped out at the way I was going overboard with my make-up, and making sure I looked my best. She woulda been talking shit about how I go all out trying to get the attention of a man, and how men ain't shit.

"We gotta get this money, and leave them niggas running behind us," she would say.

I laughed inside, and applied more foundation to my cheeks. When I heard Samuel's horn outside, I grabbed my Prada bag, and pranced to the door with my True Religion jeans feeling tighter than a muthafucka. The mirror to my left caught my attention. *Damn, J. Lo ain't got shit on me*, I thought, looking at my round ass.

Once outside, I spotted Samuel on his cell looking scrumptious. He looked my way, and motioned me to hurry to the car. I hopped inside, only to smell the best scent on a man in a long time. Hell, he smelled better than the pastor.

"Damn, you looking good, Miss Lady."

"It is what it is," I boasted. I was good at that. Being conceited was my specialty; always watched what I wore, and how I carried myself at all times. Especially this time. I crossed my legs and acted like a lady. A real lady. "So, where we headed?"

"Some place special for a special lady," he told me, in his regal voice. Strangely, he had an accent that only sounded

Caribbean every now and then. Most times his northern pitch overshadowed the Jamaican drawl that I wanted to hear more of.

His clothes looked crisp, and I could tell he had good taste by the custom made suit he wore. His mack game was on point too. I liked Samuel a lot, even coming out the gate. His style was what the doctor ordered. I hadn't been whined and dined since Carlos. I reared back in the buttery seats of his plush Bentley and smiled. It felt good being surrounded by luxury.

"You work out?" Samuel asked, salivating over my thick thighs. He turned the corner quick, but made sure to keep one of his eyes on my legs.

"Not lately, but I used to."

"I can tell." He licked his lips. "You look good, baby girl."

Damn, I'm in love, I laughed to myself. I figured I'd hype up the moment a little, so I reached over and massaged the back of his dreads with my left hand. Samuel drove faster like he enjoyed it, and turned up the sounds of Bob Marley's *'Could You Be Loved.'*

We talked like old friends all the way down the highway. He never told me where we were going, but from the sounds of his conversation when I first hopped in the car, it was something tantalizing about to pop off.

Samuel told me about how he'd been living in Atlanta for only about two years. He was originally from Jamaica, but moved to New York City with his parents over fifteen years ago. That explained why he had such an American accent.

Before I knew it, we'd whipped into a small heliport where several people with bright yellow jackets were waving us into a parking spot.

"Let's go," Samuel ordered.

Damn, a take charge man. I like. "Hold up a sec," I

replied, trying to apply a new layer of gloss to my lips.

Samuel checked his watch, and then placed his hands in his pockets. "Believe me, you look good."

"Thanks."

After finally getting out of the car, I kissed his cheek as he slid his hand around my waistline. We walked through a set of double doors, then straight to the back of what seemed to be a miniature airport. There were a few people standing around waiting, all who looked to have money. Samuel, however, carried us like we were first class.

When we got to the back of the place, a man nodded. "We've been waiting for you, Mr. McNair."

"Thanks Brother. I got held up a bit," Samuel replied.

"Oh, no problem, Sir."

"Charge it all to my card."

"Gotcha."

The man winked as he opened the door, and we were led to a small helicopter. I was in slight amazement. I felt like I'd hit the lottery. Samuel obviously had paper. I mean, real paper. Before long, we'd lifted into the air, and the pilot told us we'd have twenty-six minutes of flying time.

Samuel nodded and pulled me close to him. He got in a few free squeezes of my thighs, and I monitored his dick print, praying it was the right piece of the puzzle that was missing. Everything else was perfect; personality, looks and money.

In no time, the target was in sight. Plenty of bright lights lined the streets below. I had no idea where I was. What nearby city, what town? Nothing. This man could've been taking me off to dump me somewhere. But I didn't care. I loved every minute of it.

The helicopter landed on a pier near the water. The air was brisk, but the scenery was breathtaking. This was like a scene that should've been added in the '*Pretty Woman*' movie.

A black Limo Hummer was waiting the moment we stepped out the helicopter. I thought *damn, this shit puts Carlos to shame. Then again, who the hell is Carlos?* I laughed to myself. My smile was wide, and I'm sure Samuel could sense the excitement, but I could care less. There was no shame in my game.

"Pier Six Grill," Samuel ordered, when the driver opened the door for us.

"Got it. I'll get you there in about fifteen minutes."

When the door closed, Samuel was all over me. He wasted no time. His body was quickly positioned between my legs, and his weight forcefully had me locked with my back plunged into the seat.

"Oh, so you tryna fuck on the first date?"

He grinned and outlined my lips with his tongue. "Nah, we'll have plenty of time for that. Won't we?"

His hand lightly caressed my cheeks as he waited for an answer. It was sort of demanding, but sweet. "Won't we," he repeated.

"We sure will."

He didn't know I was game, even if we had to get down right there. I was ready to whip it on him good. Instead, he caressed my body, and kissed me hard on the lips for the entire ride. When we pulled up into the parking lot, I pushed him off a bit, to straighten my hair and fix up a little. He'd pulled my damn bra straps off after getting a few sucks on my nipples. Even when the driver opened the door, I could tell he thought we'd been fucking in the back.

As soon as we walked into the restaurant, a heavy-set waitress acted as if she'd been expecting us. Samuel gave no names, and no conversation either. The waitress politely shot him a wink, and led us to a quiet table in the back of the crowded restaurant with candles cascading about.

My new lover walked with much confidence, and I followed like his queen. We couldn't help but notice getting a few stares. Samuel ignored them, while I basked in all the attention. Hell, I wanted to be noticed. My mother said I was like this as a child. Loved to dress up, and show off. I laughed inside.

For some reason, no matter what other issues were going on in my life, rolling with Samuel was making it all better.

This was too much for me. To be in my element and living luxuriously was all I ever wanted. I didn't know much about Samuel, but he sure as hell knew how to enjoy life as far as I was concerned. My only hope was that his dick game was as tight as his mack game.

We sat down in the plush booth, and instinct told me to get close to my new man. The fact that he was four inches taller than me was a plus. On the dating scene, that didn't happen often for me. So, I nestled up under him as he held the menu with his free hand.

"You mind if I order for you?" he asked.

"Why not?" I gave up my girlish smile.

The waitress came over and brought a bottle of their finest wine. It was like Samuel never had to say a word. They all knew just how to cater to us. Before long, Samuel placed our order, and quickly turned his undivided attention to me. He looked me dead in the face and grabbed my hand, ready for a kiss. My reflex kicked in as usual. I snatched my hand back.

"Did I do something?"

"Not at all. My nails aren't done. You deserve to kiss polished nails at least." I played it off good.

Truth of the matter was that I never felt comfortable about my hands. They were rough, and too big, if you ask me. My New Year's resolution was to get paraffin waxes weekly to soften them a bit. I just hadn't followed through.

"So tell me about yourself."

"I'm single and horny," he joked

We laughed together and sipped our wine.

"No, seriously…tell me about yourself, mystery man. What do you do for a living."

"I'm an entrepreneur. I do a lil' bit of this and a lil' bit of that."

"What does all that mean? I want the simple version."

"I just gave you the only version that you need to have," he replied sharply.

His direct response caught me off guard, and I stared at him until the waitress brought a strange looking appetizer to our table, and then walked away. Everybody seemed to be on point.

"Wow, this looks good," Samuel stated, as he grabbed his spoon and scooped up the slimy object before placing it near my mouth. I guess he was waiting for me to open wide. "Try this," he said, not even giving a second thought to how rude he'd been to me.

I decided to overlook the comment, and opened wide.

"You like?" he asked.

My face frowned up, big time. "Hell no. What is it?"

"Escargot."

"Escar, what?"

"Escargot. It's a French cuisine…snails to be exact."

I wanted to throw up instantly. I grabbed my glass of wine, and took it to the head to drown the taste of dirt from my mouth.

Samuel seemed a bit frustrated. "I see we got some work to do. I don't want my woman to be a ghetto bunny, which you are for now. I want you to experience all the finer things in life."

I sat my wine glass down and thought, *Ghetto? Who the fuck are you calling ghetto?*

He kissed me again, for the ninetieth time today. I
started to say something slick back, but the sounding of my
cell phone caught me off guard. Something stupid inside of
me prompted me to answer. "Hello," I scrambled to get the
phone to my ear.

"Who is this?" I questioned. The voice on the other
end was familiar. At first I thought it was my brother calling
back. I really did miss him being in my life, but now wasn't a
good time. "Jerell, is that you?" I questioned.

"You wanna make some money?"

"Who is this?" I asked with a frown.

"It's Pastor Scott. Meet me at the club at 11p.m."

How the fuck did he get my cell phone number? Then it
dawned on me. *That bitch Essence*. "I can't." I inched away
from Samuel, hoping he couldn't hear any part of the conversation.

"Tell 'em you're with me," Samuel interrupted. His island tone emerged more than ever before.

My daze grew stronger. This nigga was completely
sure of himself. "It's an old friend," I said, covering the phone
with my hand.

"I'm sure. Get off the phone," he demanded, in a softer
tone than normal.

"Look, we'll have to hook up tomorrow." I ended the
conversation quickly.

"So, what is it that you do?" Samuel asked.

I thought about giving him a smart-ass version now
that the tables had turned, but decided not to respond. Instead,
I moved closer, and damn near sucked his tongue out of his
mouth.

Chapter Nine

If looks could kill, I'd be dead. From every shuttle bus driver who passed by, to even the police directing traffic away from the curb, my body made them all catch the vapors. Little did they know that if my baby pulled up on 'em, they'd be in trouble.

Samuel had rushed off to cop us a limo ride from the airport service desk, and told me to wait curbside, patiently and *quietly* until he returned. *Quietly*, I wanted to say. But, I just folded my arms, cut my eyes and smiled.

Although we'd spent every other night together over the last two weeks, spending the last week with Samuel in Detroit, where we never left each other's sight, gave me a chance to get to know him a little better. Learning his style, his mannerisms, and every twitch of his dick kept me moist. It seemed like we'd fucked fifty times in just five days. We'd shop, then fuck. Eat, then fuck. Sleep, then fuck. The only problem was, a bitch had to get used to his jealous issues.

Supposedly, he'd gone with me to Detroit to support me when I appeared in court for the credit card fraud charges. Instead of support, that negro broke bad with the lawyer he paid for. Samuel accused him of gawking at my tits. Mr. Caberra quit on the spot, and left my ass standing before the judge with my jaw hanging low.

Somehow, Samuel got word to the prosecutor during the short recess, and my case was ironically dismissed. The prosecutor said they didn't have enough evidence. I thought it was strange, but who cared. Whenever Samuel got involved with anything, he always seemed to know exactly what to do. I felt so safe and protected with him, but his domineering nature was fifty percent enjoyable, fifty percent fear.

Besides, the way he was spending money on me, made me forget about all his flaws. Just about the same time that I saw an older model black limo whip the corner, my cell rang. I started not to answer, but when I saw Essence's number, I decided to pick up. I'd been calling her for days while away, and gotten no answer.

When the limo pulled up, I squinted, trying to catch a glimpse of anyone through the deeply tinted windows. I wasn't sure if the car was for us, so I stayed on the curb just to be sure, as Essence's irritated voice blared through the phone.

"Hello. I said hello!" she shouted.

"I hear you." I still kept my eyes on the parked limo.

"Look, I got your message. I thought you said your flight got in at eight?"

"Essence, how dare you, heifer! I been ringing your damn phone off the hook for days. And now you wanna call me and ask me when I'm coming home?"

Samuel emerged from the airport terminal with an attitude. His eyes revealed that he was upset. He was talking on his cell too, so not many words were exchanged between the two of us. Even though my eyes followed his wave, I couldn't help but admire the way he was dressed for the tenth time that day. That was how my man rolled. His grey colored slacks and black Giorgio Armani pullover shirt was casual, yet fit for a king. It read expensive. Better yet, everything about him was always done in good taste.

Essence continued to rant like she was my man, as the driver finally stepped out to usher us into the car and grabbed our bags.

"Look chicka, you been acting real funky lately. You had any dick lately, girlie?" I asked. ""Cause you need some."

She obviously didn't think it was funny.

"No, bitch. You need some real dick!" she shouted. "You riding around playing house with that fake-ass Jamaican, missing out on a lot of green."

"Oh no, honey. I'm getting mine."

I wanted to say more, but as Samuel spoke into his cell phone, his eyes were glued to my lips. He watched every motion of my mouth, and probably knew how many cavities I had by now. It was slightly frightful, but he'd told me before that he enjoyed studying every inch of my body. I grinned and kept talking in codes.

"Anyway, how far you away?"

"Ahh...lemme check with Samuel."

Before I could ask him, he smashed his index finger against my lips, summonsing me to be quiet. *I'm on a business call*, he mouthed.

"Ahh...I should be home in about thirty minutes," I uttered to Essence.

"Good. Be sure to bring that man of yours upstairs when you get here. I got something real important to discuss with him."

I had no idea what Essence wanted to talk to Samuel about, and wasn't in the mood to deal with her attitude, so her meeting would have to wait

"Bet," I lied, as I closed my flip phone and stared at my man.

He was such a hot-head and quick to blow his temper. I'd seen him lose control during phone calls, and once even started banging the phone into the ground, and stomping whatever was nearby. Still in all, I was falling hard for his raging personality.

Samuel was laid back in his seat leaning to the side like a sho nuff gangster. The way he twisted his words on his phone conversation, told me something shady was up with him. But the moment he flashed his dimples over at me, I dismissed the idea of anything suspicious going on. After all, while we were in Detroit, Samuel told me that he was a real-estate mogul. What harm could come from buying and selling properties?

I waited patiently a few more minutes for Samuel to end his business call. The divider between us and the driver was up, so a little play time was in order. I reached over and slid my hand back and forth across his crotch. He widened his legs so I could get my free feels. Immediately his manhood hardened as I stroked his trapped meat.

Samuel looked over at me with those dark eyes, not once pausing during his telephone conversation. I gave him a seductive grin and batted my eyes, as if to say, *give me some of that*.

Surprisingly, Samuel grabbed my wrist, and stopped me just as I was about to unzip his pants.

"You know the deal," he said.

At first I thought he was talking to me. Then I realized he was talking to the person on the line.

"Look brotha, I made myself clear. Have all my money on Thursday."

I wasn't used to rejection, so I was deeply into my feelings. First, because he wouldn't let me service him with the best head in Atlanta. Secondly, because he was treating me like I wasn't his first priority. Whoever was on the line had him in a heated conversation. Money seemed to be on the line, but I didn't give a fuck. I wanted some sexy shit to jump off on our ride to Essence's place.

Noticing my attitude, Samuel reached down between my legs, parting my thighs in my short Chloe skirt, and began to massage my clit. My panties got wet immediately. I threw my head back on the seat, and closed my eyes in anticipation. Samuel had been sexing me to death for days, so I was more than anxious. I could still hear him handling business on the phone, not realizing until I opened my eyes slightly that he was on the floor of the limo.

"Baby, what are you doing?" I asked in a whisper.

He put his finger to his lips for me to be quiet, while he used the other hand to keep his cell phone in contact with his ear.

His accent seemed to deepen again, "Well, it seems like I'll have to handle this differently if that's the case."

Samuel pushed my legs further apart, slid my thong to the side, and gently licked my clit; all with the phone still to his ear. I could hear the muffled conversation of the caller on the other end.

As he began to suck my clit, I trembled. He had a tight hold of it, causing my legs to shake uncontrollably. I brought my left leg up, bending it at the knee, and my four and a half inch Jimmy Choo stiletto heel pierced the leather seats.

Samuel took a breath from between my thighs to end his call, "You know what it is," he spoke sternly. After finally closing his phone, and tossing it to the empty seat, he continued to feast on my pussy. "Chanel, baby you taste so good. You know this is my pussy, right?"

Between breaths, I moaned, "Yes, baby it's all yours."

"Don't ever cross me, Chanel," he said sensually.

I won't baby. Sssssssss…" I hissed. "I-I-I-I-I won't."

Samuel put the tongue game down. With his thumb and pointer finger he separated my lips, giving full exposure to my clit. He blew cool air softly directly onto it, 'causing it to stand at attention like a pink rose bud. Gently he sucked it, and then licked it, as his pace increased, and the sucking intensified. I could feel my juices seeping out, causing the leather seat to get wet and sticky.

Samuel ate my pussy like it was an art.

"Girl, I want you to cum right here in my mouth. I

want to suck the cum from this good pussy."

I could barely speak, but managed to respond, "O-o-k-k-kay, baby. S-s-s-s, damn that shit feels good. Keep working it right there."

Samuel drove his tongue deep into my wetness. My juices greeted him with delight. I couldn't resist grabbing his head full of locks, pushing him closer into my vagina. As he slipped two fingers in my clean-shaven garden, his tongue found its way to my ass. Darting in and out quickly, matching the rhythm of his fingers that penetrated my pussy.

"Fuck this tongue, baby. Cum on my face. Yeah, girl fuck this tongue."

My back began to arch, as I could feel my explosion coming to the surface. His fingers were slightly bent in my pussy, hitting my G spot, as his tongue danced on my clit. Losing all control, my body began to spasm uncontrollably, while I managed to hold his head tightly on the target. My juices exploded onto Samuel's face as my body began to relax. He started licking me clean when my fears got the best of me. I'd just remembered I hadn't given him the finger test. *Damn, what the fuck was I thinking!*

Instantly, I jumped on Samuel, like a hungry bear. He could sense I wanted more, yet little did he know it was all a trick. I massaged his balls and yanked his pants down, ready to go down south. There wasn't much time to be wasted, so my mouth darted to the target.

The moment I started sucking, his eyes closed slightly, with his head titled to the side. Samuel moaned and groaned, while I sucked and mentally fucked. I had him in the zone as I prepared to administer the test.

I'd been taught years ago, that if a man let you slip two fingers into his asshole, and didn't whip your ass, he just might be gay. I'd had my bout with undercover gay brothers, so Samuel had to get the test. He looked like a real man, and he damn sho felt like one when stickin' it to me, but only time would tell.

I continued licking him like a lollipop, while massaging his balls at the same time. My hands were nice and warm, so as my left hand worked up a sweat, my right massaged Samuel's golden-colored ass cheek. He squirmed a bit, probably uncomfortable with his position, 'cause I had him spread eagle on the seat with his knees six inches apart. The more he tried to tighten them, the more I pushed his legs apart.

When I realized Samuel's eyeballs were rolling into the back of his eyelids, I made my move. My two fingers to the right of my thumb were massive, so I even screeched the minute my fingers touched his asshole.

Samuel wasted no time with his reaction. The moaning sounds came to an instant halt, as he lifted slightly from the seat, and back slapped me so hard that I flew backwards into the seat on the other side of the limo.

"What the fuck is up with you?"

"Umm...nothing baby. Just trying to give you some kinky loving that's all," I responded, holding my throbbing cheek. In a way, I guess I deserved the slap.

"Don't be trying to put your damn fingers in my ass!"

So much for being gay, I thought. "I'm sorry. I thought you would like it."

"What kind of man likes that type of shit?" he asked. "As a matter of fact, I'll show you some kinky loving since you wanna play."

He dove on top of me instantly, and commenced to giving it to me rough. We tussled our way into different positions for the next twenty minutes, fucking like we'd never fucked before. He tried his best to hit it from the back, but I wasn't having it. I wanted it long-stroke-style. He obliged, giving me all eight juicy inches. Eventually, he nutted, and I lay there limp and exhausted from being turned the fuck out.

By the time the limo slowed its pace, we were pulling in front of my temporary home. I could barely see through the deeply tinted windows, but hoped no one could see me while I fixed my clothes back to perfection. When the limo driver yanked the door open, a slight breeze helped to dilute the sex filled odor.

"Did you have a comfortable ride, Mr. Anderson?"

"Absolutely," Samuel responded with a smile.

The driver wore a slight grin, almost as if he knew we'd been banging. I had a blank expression written all over my face. On our first date, I clearly remember Samuel being called Mr. McNair at the heliport. Now, this driver called him Mr. Anderson. When we flew to Detroit, his ticket said Blackmon. *Who is this fuckin' guy?* I wondered.

I looked around for a hidden camera or sound device. Muthafuckas crazy in the world these days, so I didn't rule anything out. My body inched slowly past Samuel, since he obviously wasn't getting out.

"You gon' see me to the door?" I asked with attitude.

"Of course, I wouldn't send a beautiful woman like you to the door alone. Jeffrey will take care of you," he answered, then licked the side of my cheek. "I've got an important business call to make." He whipped out a stack of bills, and handed me a few hundreds. "This should hold you."

I smiled. "When will I see you again?"

"Soon." He grinned. He blew me several kisses, and started talking into his cell.

I looked at Jeffrey like he was beneath me, and pranced to the door, while he followed with my bags.

When we reached the apartment door, I gave him a snooty nod, that said drop the bags and get the fuck away from the door. He looked like he wanted a tip, but I knew my baby would take care of him when he got back to the car. I didn't even stick my key in the door until I saw him take his first two steps back down the staircase.

When I turned the top lock and pushed the door open, a strange scent hit me in the face. It was familiar, yet intimidating. I used my feet to help nudge my bags through the door. All along my eyes widened at the scenery. Candles were lit everywhere, then suddenly music softly began to play. Maybe this was a set up? Perhaps Samuel had asked Essence to prepare it all?

Nice, I thought, as I took mini steps through the living room area. Suddenly, Essence appeared wearing an all leather corset, and gripping a long black whip in her left hand. Instantly my body froze.

While my face tightened, my mind raced. Didn't Essence know I didn't have feelings for her?

"Look, Essence. We gotta talk." My head shook from right to left like a speeding tennis ball. My opposition showed.

She moved closer with warm intentions. Lustful intentions. Hell, I wasn't moved. I'd just had my pussy eaten like I was a piece of watermelon by a gorgeous man with bulging biceps…and he'd passed the finger test. I grinned at the thought.

Essence snuck me good. She rolled up on me, and wrapped her full lips around my mouth. Quickly, I stepped back. My eyes damn near popped out my head. She was ready for the get down, and I was in shock. I thought about fainting, until the obvious darted from the corner of the kitchen. My hands quickly scrubbed my eyes. I had to be dreaming…I prayed.

The pastor stood half-naked in a matching black and gold bikini-bathing suit. He stroked his dick with one hand, and pulled strands of hair from his wig with the other. Our eyes locked momentarily, then Essence waved him closer.

What the fuck is going on around here, I thought.

"See, we been waiting for you," she uttered.

I backed away, headed for the door 'cause I damn sho wasn't about to get caught up in their little threesome party.

However, the moment I turned, Tiger appeared behind me, and grabbed me by my waist. I felt her bare skin against my stomach, and completely lost it. I twirled into a complete three sixty, ready to fight, stab, or whatever I had to do. Although Tiger was completely naked, she seemed to be the least threatening. Her mouth remained wide open, as if she needed to be told what to do next. The pastor who, licked his lips full of bright red lipstick, scared me the most. I'd been involved in some wild shit in life, but his cross-dressing performance went over the top. I closed my eyes, screamed, and pretended it wasn't happening.

Chapter Ten

"Bitch, do you hear what I'm saying to you?" Essence blared.

I ignored her every word, and just kept stuffing my shit into my faithful Louie Vuitton duffel bags. My clothes were crumbled on top of the futon, and were flying in all directions, but everything had to go. There were no chances of me coming back, homeless or not. Luckily, all my new gear, compliments of Samuel, was still packed neatly in the shopping bags, so just a few more minutes, and I'd be done. Done with Essence for good.

"So, what you not talking to me?" Essence's voice deepened. "You didn't say shit last night, and said we'd talk about it in the morning. Well, bitch, it's morning," she said, snatching the curtains back, and allowing the bright-ass sunlight to come in.

I still said nothing.

"Oh, so you gon' trip on me!"

Enough was enough. Essence had crossed the line. Bringing Pastor Scott to our house, and trying that ol' orgy bullshit was more than I was willing to put up with. Tiger, Essence, and the pastor; all too much. It didn't matter anymore. The fact remained, I'd now become a one-woman-man.

"Look, Essence. I appreciate you letting me stay, but your ass crossed the line with that dumb shit last night. I mean...you had the pastor dressed up like Tootsie, and Tiger just following your crazy-ass lead. Anything you say, she'll do."

"Look, trick!" She smiled. Then waited for me to return the grin. I didn't. "You know I wasn't tryna hurt you. I thought we'd been over this a thousand times. I just wanted to calm your feisty ass down. Besides, you was rude as hell, and I forgave you."

"Forgave me for what?" I snapped.

Essence's cell phone rang which instantly saved her ass from getting cursed out. After answering, she said a few words, then shouted, "Hold the fuck on!" into the phone before laying it back down. Quickly, she got right back in my face. "Chanel, I had to tell my company to leave last night because you was up in here breaking up all my shit." She paused. "Which you will pay for later. But, I made them leave, didn't I? All for your ass."

"Sam will be here in a minute, and I'on want no trouble," I warned.

"Trouble? Am I supposed to be scared? That Jamaican looking nigga don't put no fucking fear in my heart."

She trembled, trying make a joke of my comment. But I was dead serious. I'd seen him get ugly. Plus, I'd heard him make threats over the phone that sounded like they'd soon turn to promises.

"Go 'head, have fun." I pressed my last sweater into the bag and struggled to zip it shut.

"I tried to make you happy Chanel!"

"Look, Essence, you should've told me you wanted me before I moved in here. I thought we were girls. I was never looking for love. Besides, I ain't no dike."

She folded her arms. "Could've fooled me. I see the way you look at Stacy."

"Whatever." I waved her ass off. "Stacy's my girl…and you used to be."

Before I could turn around, Essence had grabbed my wrist from behind. "Whatcha gon' do about your debt?"

"I breathed hard. "Get off of me, now!" I gritted my

teeth, but didn't move. It was no need for a fight. Besides, I was more than sure that I could kick her ass with no problem.

"Answer the question." She squeezed tighter.

"What? Are you crazy? Get the fuck off of me!" I yelled. "I'm serious, Essence."

"Oh, I'm serious too. You owe me for soap, use of toilet tissue, electricity, and eating up my damn food. Shiii-itttttttt, I aughta charge yo ass a penalty for leaving early." She laughed crazily. "Oh, and don't forget $500 for breaking up all my Lenox dishes last night, and $300 for breaking my mother's vase."

"Whether you know it or not, I did you a favor!"

Quickly, I jerked away, catching her off guard. With my new oversized Fendi purse in sight, I grabbed my bags, threw my purse over my shoulder, and headed to the front door.

"Oh, Chanel, you forgot these!" she shouted, shaking the small prescription bottle.

My heart skipped a beat. My pills I needed, so I put my game face on. I turned toward Essence with a slight smile, "Thanks, girl...and no hard feelings, okay?" I said, walking toward her to grab the bottle.

Instantly, Essence snatched the bottle away as soon as my hand was within reach. "Stop playing games, Essence. I gotta go."

"Go 'head, trick. I'ma hold these til you pay up."

Something in her eyes told me she knew what was up. Remaining calm was the key. It had to be done. The pills were a necessity.

"Shit," I said to myself. "Look, girl, whatever I owe you, I got you."

"Sure. I got you too," she responded, with a smirk. "You think I don't know what's up?"

I shrugged my shoulders with worry in my eyes.

"Essence. I'm not sure what you're trying to prove, but I don't have time for this." I tried to grab the bottle again, but she snatched her hand away.

"Let's walk out together and tell ol' Sammy boy about these mufuckin' pills."

Everything went black. All I could hear were the pills moving around in the bottle. They sounded foul just like my world. Everything was being shaken up. My second chance at love, and now Essence wanted to fuck it up.

I dropped my bags to the floor, and rushed my deranged roommate like a fuming linebacker. Her bark was always strong, but her bite was weak. I was stronger, angrier, and had a lot more to lose. Her fearful expression showed that she knew this would end messy.

We tussled back and forth like two inmates on the yard. Me on top of her, then she on top of me. My grip was strong, but Essence had a bit of fight remaining.

"It was supposed to be me and you," she uttered. "We could've been good together."

I never spoke a word. I had to win. I tugged at her hands wrapped tightly around the bottle, while pinning her to the wooden kitchen table. At the same time my defeat was near, my phone rang distracting me. My heart raced even more. *Samuel,* I thought. I reached for my purse, while maintaining my grip on Essence's neck. She couldn't move much, but her wicked grin remained.

Within moments, I managed to grab my purse, reached inside for my phone, and stumbled onto my razor. The phone sounded again. This time over and over again.

"Let the bottle go Essence!" I roared.

"Hell no. I'll give 'em to Samuel…"

That was it. *Did she say Samuel?* I couldn't take but so much. *No more would be tolerated*, I told myself. I'd come too far to let a bitch like Essence get in my way, so with a flick of my wrist, I snapped. My razor popped out, and commenced to slicing Essence's neck.

Chapter Eleven

Seven days later, I was still in shock. Too much anguish had gone on in my life. I sat up in the oversized luxury bed, ready for a drink, a new habit that had been brewing over the last few days. My life had been turned completely upside down. Why? I wasn't sure, 'cause Samuel had been by my side day in and day out. He knew my feelings about the Essence situation, but he assured me, I'd be straight if he ran the show.

So, instead of crying and sulking, we dined in the lapse of luxury, and he provided me with everything a girl could want. Still in all, emotionally, I was drained. And physically, just plain exhausted.

None of that mattered to Samuel, 'cause like clockwork he wanted his pussy served sunny side up in the morning, and fried sizzling hot just before bed.

We'd been fucking ferociously every day for the last seven days since I left Essence's place running like hell. For Samuel, it was perfect. He didn't care that I felt like I was on the run. He had me just where he wanted me; in his bed daily. His instant housewife is what he called it.

I hadn't even been to the club to work, 'cause he was totally against it. "No woman of mine is gonna be shaking her ass in front of no other man," he'd say, with dominance in his voice. I sat back and took it, 'cause I didn't want to be kicked out of his gorgeous-ass lake front house in Covington.

Suddenly, my thoughts were interrupted as Samuel

moaned, stretching his hairy arms above his head, and ending with a tight clutch on my pussy. His next move was predictable. *This man loves to fuck*, I thought. He hadn't even opened his eyes good, and his dick was already at attention.

"Good morning, sexy."

"Morning, boo." I managed to let a smile slip through the side of my mouth. "You got in a little late last night, didn't you?"

"Baby, how many times I gotta tell you, let a man be a man. Don't I take good care of you?" he asked, massaging my clit.

I nodded. He was surely telling the truth. "It's just that I was lonely last night, baby. You know I got a lot on my mind."

His heavy hands moved in a more vigorous motion. It was damn sho turning me on, but I had to get my point across. "What's with you leaving out anyway, after getting these mysterious calls? And at 2 a.m. in the morning, at that?"

Samuel jumped up onto both knees, and straddled his body above me quickly. His eyes were different. Scary. Frightening, yet still loveable. He grabbed me by the bottom of my chin with force and squeezed tightly, bringing his lips to meet mine. His words were soft spoken, yet so sincere.

"Listen, I run this muthafuckin show. Now, don't let your sexy ass forget that." He licked the side of my face softly.

I sat frozen, unwilling to even speak.

"You wanna wear the pants?"

"Ahh…no. That's what I got you for." I tried to make light of the situation.

"Then stay in your place, and lemme make you feel good. Lemme take care of you like you supposed to be taken care of. Now, from time to time, I might have to roll out at 4 a.m., but just know I'm rolling out for us. We gotta eat, right?"

I tried to nod my agreement, but Samuel's tongue held my mouth captive. His juices danced around my mouth, in an attempt to get me horny. It just wasn't happening. In some strange way, it seemed as if Samuel had a mind of his own, along with his mesmerizing body parts. He only wanted to address issues that were important to him, and only when the fuck he wanted to discuss them!

Sure, his controlling nature had been obvious to me from our first date, but day by day, it was getting stranger and scarier. I wanted to love Samuel for the rest of my life, but out of affection, not fear.

Soon enough, Samuel's grip loosened from my chin, and his pelvic area began to grind harder on top of me. Today, for the first time, I couldn't even get wet below. Yet tears streamed from my eyes freely. Samuel never stopped grinding, but the touch of his forefinger wiping away my tears told me he cared.

"So, why you crying, pretty lady?"

"No reason."

"No reason? Now I don't believe that. Tell me, sexy. You can tell me anything."

"I guess it's just all that's been happening to me. First the situation with my parents, then Essence, now you."

"Me? What have I done? Other than treat you like a queen?"

"That's just it. I'm just so happy to have you. I'ma be honest, it's 20 to 1 out there. Finding a man these days is hard."

"Is that so?" he asked, in between kisses. "Well, I'm one hundred percent yours, and that shouldn't make you cry. It should make you happy."

"I am happy. You're the first thing that feels right to come into my life in a long time. So don't fuck it up." I pressed my body into his, ready to return his grinds. "I'm yours for life, right? Mr. McNair, Anderson, Blackmon, or whoever you are today."

Samuel quickly lifted his body away from me. He looked as if he needed time to think. He'd finally developed a deeper puzzled look when he asked, "What's all that talk you doing?"

"It's just that I wanna know who I'm loving. What's your real name?"

"Samuel Blackmon," he uttered, without hesitation.

"Then what are the other names all about? You know I'm far from stupid. I grew up with a hip brother."

He laughed. "From time to time, I use different alias to keep me safe. Keep people outta my business. Nothing to worry your pretty lil' head about though."

I nodded, but my alter ego gave me a wake up call inside. Hell, I had alias too…and it wasn't for protection. I was into criminal activities. I'm sure he was too. Samuel was into something shady. I knew it, but I loved him, with his sneakiness and all.

"I just want us to work," I confessed to my man.

Just as I was spilling my guts to the man I'd fallen hard for, his phone rang and diverted his attention.

"Yo," Samuel blared into the phone. A phone that he kept near him at all times. It almost seemed glued to his body.

He managed to flip over me and wrap the sheet around his body in a matter of seconds. "What the fuck?" he shouted. "Uh huh…Uh huh."

I listened intently, 'cause something was definitely up. My body moved closer to his, as if we still needed to cuddle, but Samuel was no fool. He moved further away to have as much privacy as possible.

"Bet. Be there in thirty," he said, ending his call.

"In thirty?" I questioned, with an attitude.

"Yeah, in thirty. You gotta problem with that?"

I looked downward, never saying another word about him having to leave. I sat in bed like a mental patient, watching Samuel throw on some jeans and an oversized beige Polo shirt. It was so unlike him not to be dressed to perfection. His casual attire verified that something urgent was calling for his quick attention. Samuel headed my way, as he swooped his dreads behind his back, and tied with a thick rubber band. He knelt down on one knee and hit me with a soft smile.

"I'll be back soon. You want me to bring you anything to eat?"

"No need. Stacy is gonna come pick me up around 11 o'clock. She's taking me to pick up my last check from Big Willy."

Samuel's entire expression changed. "I thought we discussed you and the club?" he asked firmly.

"We did. And…that's why I'm not working there anymore."

"I'll tell you what. I'll swing by there and get your check. Tell Stacy to fall back. You my woman. I got all your needs taken care of. And you know what else…"

"What?" I asked, looking like a lonely child who couldn't go out and play.

"Tonight I'm taking you out. I'ma show you what real clubbing is all about. My boy is having a party down at the Platinum. When I get back, I'll take you shopping to get something spectacular. Be ready. I wanna show you off to the world."

I cracked a smile and blew him a kiss. Shopping was the one word that would always put a smile on my face and make me forget anything else...good or bad. Samuel headed out the door, as I pulled the covers over my head. I had to find a way to tell Stacy I was grounded and couldn't hang out with her for the day.

***

By the time evening rolled around, I'd put aside my attitude, and sat in front of the 60 inch plasma in the living room drinking like a drunken sailor, and looking like I was about to prance down a runway at a fashion show. Absolute and cranberry juice had become my favorite drink. One to start off my day, and two or three more would be downed by the end of the night. Life was rough. Too much to contemplate; always worried about getting caught, or found out. So, I kicked my six-hundred dollar Manolo Blahnik peep-toe heels onto the top of the ottoman and took my drink to the head. I smiled inside at the smoothness of the taste going down. It was the only thing that gave me peace.

While I waited patiently for Samuel to come take me on my shopping spree at Lenox Square Mall, my mind drifted off into another world. I thought about how many women would love to walk in my shoes. The fact that I was now living with Samuel in a custom built seven bedroom house that looked like something off of MTV Cribs. Nine foot cathedral ceilings graced the house from the bottom to the top; along with a gourmet kitchen and granite countertops. I remember the first day my feet crossed the threshold to the front door. The fabulous spiral staircase extending from the foyer won me over. The open space with cascading high-priced chandeliers, confirmed that his spot was the place for me. This was the life I'd always wanted for myself, and now that I got it, something just didn't seem right about my fairytale world.

I jumped up from my trance when I heard the sound of the front door closing. I straightened my skirt, and snapped the clasp to my heels quickly, dying to get to the mall.

When Samuel entered the room with a Neiman Marcus bag in hand, my facial expression changed. I had a dumb-

founded look as I stood frozen in the middle of the floor.
Samuel just watched me closely for a few moments before
speaking.

"Don't I always treat my baby good," he said proudly.
He held out his arms, showing off the bags.

"I thought *we* were going to the mall." I put so much
emphasis on we that I knew he didn't like it.

"Damn it!" he shouted. "A brother can't even surprise
his woman! What the fuck!"

Samuel always spoke slower than most men I'd dated.
It was part of his unique sounding voice. But the way he ac-
centuated his words extra slowly put a little fear in my heart.

"Oh no…it's cool, baby. I just thought we were going
together. Show me whatchu' got. I know you got good taste.
Forgive me. I'm just stressed and ready to go out. Let's go
have a good time tonight. Okay."

"That's my girl." He grinned, and pulled out a short
black Marc Jacobs dress with thin spaghetti straps and ready
made push up cushions, something I didn't need.

My face tightened but my mouth managed to do the
right thing. "Thanks," I finally said. "I love it."

"Really?"

"Yeah…really."

It was cute, I thought to myself, but nothing I
would've picked out on my own. Freak-um dresses were my
favorite, but I wanted the kind that made my ass sit up a little
more. I'd spent a lot of money maintaining my good looks, so
showing off was a necessity.

"What time we leaving?" I asked with as much enthu-
siasm as I could.

"About nine."

"Bet. I have time to wash my hair, so I can look really
good for you."

I blew him a kiss and headed upstairs to the master

bathroom. Since moving in, Samuel had pretty much turned the master bath over to me, 'cause of my tons of cosmetics and toiletries. Good thing though, cause I really needed a quiet, secluded place in the house where I could be alone. My own place; my personal sanctuary. Just like he had, in his forbidden bedroom. It was the bedroom to the left of ours. He kept it locked at all times, and told me it was simply his space.

Walking past his secret room made me wanna kick the door down. All of a sudden flashbacks of Essence lying on the floor with blood goosing from her neck invaded my mind. Emotionally, I was having another breakdown. I was just good at pretending it wasn't happening.

As soon as I swung the bathroom door open, I grabbed my pills from my secret spot beneath the far left cabinet, and popped a pill from each of the three bottles. When I turned the faucet on to cup some water into the palm of my hand, the image of myself in the mirror startled me. *Was I really happy? I wondered, and at what expense?*

***

Hours had gone by. My weave smelled good, looked good, and the tresses that flowed down my back couldn't be fucked with. Tonight I was gonna be the best looking broad Samuel had ever carried on his arm. I lingered in the bathroom a few more minutes, putting the final touches on my make-up. I could hear Samuel calling me from downstairs, but I pretended not to hear him. My cheek bones glistened the more I stroked my bronzing powder across them. I had to make sure everything was perfect, so that I'd feel good about myself, and walk out the house with a smile.

When I opened the bathroom door, three vases full of red roses sat on top of the marble topped dresser. My head darted to the left, searching for Samuel. I figured he'd want to see the look on my face. He really was a sweet guy, in spite of his temper and controlling behavior. I lifted the card off the first vase and beamed at the message- *I'll make you mine forever real soon*.

Damn, does that mean what I think it does, I thought. I pulled my hair off my neck, and headed downstairs with a wide grin. When I approached the bottom step, my sexy man was standing there with his hands in his pocket like we were headed to the prom.

As always, he looked handsome in his black Hugo Boss slacks and fancy mauve colored shirt with embroidered sleeves and diamond cuff links. Between his good looks and suave personality, I could only imagine how many tricks were after my man.

When my feet touched the marble tiled foyer, he reached out for my hand. I stepped down like I was the shit, grabbed his hand, and allowed him to lead me to the car. It had been a while since I really acted like a lady or was treated like one. Samuel was just what the doctor ordered.

"Thanks for the flowers," I finally said.

"No doubt. Now hop in, pretty lady."

I smiled when I saw the Absolute and cranberry to go sitting in the cup holder. Samuel didn't approve of me over-doing it with the drinks, so I knew he wanted me to relax for the night and have a good time.

Within minutes, we'd gotten into the car and made our way out of our exclusive neighborhood of Lyndhurst. We did-n't talk much, 'cause Samuel had the music pumping. The Bose system was loud, and sounding like we were front row at the concert. It got me pumped instantly. My head was bob-bing like crazy to R. Kelly and Biggie's, *'Fucking you Tonight.'* I sipped my drink then sung along…*You must be used to me spending, and all that sweet wining and din-ing…well I'm fucking you tonight…here's another one…and another one.*

"Oh yeah," I said to Samuel and smiled.

He returned the smile and bobbed his head too as the beats infiltrated the car. I was feeling good, so I sang along with Biggie, like I was gonna be doing the dick slinging. *"Some say the x make the sex spectacular, let me lick you from yo neck to yo back, then ya shivering, tongue delivering, chills up that spine, that ass is mine. Skip the wine and the candlelight. No Cristal tonight. If it's alright with you...we fucking."*

I laughed and rubbed Samuel on the back of his neck. He just grinned and kept singing. Damn, that shit had me so hyped, I couldn't wait to get to the club to order me another Absolute and cranberry juice, but even stronger this time.

I laughed, thinking about how crazy I had become. Then, all of a sudden my laughter was cut short. I saw how Samuel had stopped bobbing his head, and constantly checked his rear-view mirror. So like clockwork, I checked mine too. I wasn't sure if we were seeing the same thing, so I kept quiet and just observed.

The more I watched, the more I noticed a black Impala dipping in and out of traffic, five to six cars behind us. Samuel was cool about it though. He made a sharp turn onto North Druid Hills Road, then a sharp left onto Bridgeporth. I assumed just to see if the car was really following us.

Sure enough, the Impala was still trailing behind. Next thing I knew, Samuel had put the pedal to the medal. He was zooming down the highway, going ninety miles per hour in a residential neighborhood. I yanked my seatbelt across my lower body, hoping it would save my life when we crashed, 'cause he was definitely on some do or die shit.

"Who do you think it is, honey?" I asked, becoming a little more nervous.

"Chill!" he shouted.

I shut up and tried to remain calm. My focus switched to the side view mirror. I knew I had to be a down ass chick, but hell, I didn't know if we was about to get robbed or what. Next thing I knew, Samuel had reached beneath his seat and pulled out a nine millimeter.

"What the fuck? You never told me you had a gun?"

"I never told you a lot, sweetheart. Now shut the fuck up, so I can lose these bastards."

I sat with a grim look on my face. I wanted answers. I needed answers. Hell, I deserved an explanation. Before I knew it, we'd gotten back onto North Druid Hills Road, without any black cars in sight. And within minutes, we'd hopped onto highway 85.

Samuel turned the music back up, slid his gun back under the seat, and bobbed his head like nothing had ever happened. No explanation, no baby, I'm sorry. No, that was somebody I knew from back in the day. No, oh they was probably trying to rob us. Nothing!

"Who in the hell am I dealing with?" I mouthed softly to myself .

I just kept looking at Samuel. He looked like he was thinking, *hard*. I started to dig into his ass, to see what was up, but when he gripped my hand, I cut him some slack.

"You okay," I asked?"

"Oh, I'm straight. You know young niggas these days see you in a nice ride like this, and try to get at'cha. I got my gat under the seat, so we gon' be okay, always."

"You sure that's what that was all about?"

He nodded, so I said no more. Twenty more minutes passed as we rode without conversation. No talking at all, only music. Music that had me hyped. Music that made me wanna shake my ass. I had already decided that I wasn't gonna let that little weird driving episode destroy my night. The moment we pulled up to the valet stand at Club Platinum,

I popped open my car door.

"Chanel, be a lady. Wait for the attendant to open the door," Samuel instructed.

"Oh, I forgot. I'm just ready to have a good time."

"And you will." He looked at me sternly, and grabbed my hand tightly.

When we entered the dimly lit club the music was pumping. '*Get Money*' by Junior Mafia filled the air. I loved that old school music. I danced my way to the VIP section, trailing Samuel like a puppy. The club was live, and party goers filled the room, but I couldn't help cutting my eyes at a tall dark-skinned brother who'd walked in shortly after us, and now stood babysitting the bar.

His head was completely shaved and his pearly white teeth glistened as he smiled a long smile to my backside. I tried to ignore him, but there was something striking about him. He continued to watch my every move, so I decided to hold on tight to my man, before he caught a glimpse and got the wrong impression.

By the time we made it to the back of the club, there was a round booth with five bottles of Moet covering the table.

"All this for us?" I asked, as Samuel escorted me to the center of the booth.

It was a crazy feeling, almost a sense of, *here you go. This is your spot for the night, so stay put. Like hell*, I thought to myself. I'm gonna have a good damn time tonight.

"Order me an Absolute and cranberry," I quickly told Samuel, while moving to the beat of the music.

"We drinking bottles tonight," he replied. "Nothing but the best for my baby."

"But…"

"Look, I know what's good for you."

Hated it, I thought. "But…"

"Shhh…" He placed his index finger over my lips, just as two short, well dressed guys approached the table. They looked so serious, not at all like they came out for a good time. At first I thought it was a hit like one of the club scenes in the movie, '*Scarface*', until Samuel stood up with confidence and shook the hand of the shortest guy.

"Les, my man. Long time no see," Samuel said.

"What's good?"

"You. Money Making Sam," they all joked.

They both nodded at me when he introduced me as his lady, and sat down on the two ends of the booth. Instantly, the shortest guy, who had a tan like he'd been baked in the sun, had his eyes glued to the center of my chest. Hell, I knew my tits popped out as soon as you saw me, but damn.

Before I knew it, we were all getting more attention than I expected. It didn't take long for me to realize that these guys were balling, and the regulars in the club knew it. Ladies passed by far too much with seductive comments, interested in their free drinks for the night. I sat quietly, watched intensely, and danced in my seat all by my lonesome, while Samuel quickly got down to business, and secretly discussed some strange business deal across the table.

The more he whispered into the ear of the shorter guy who he called 'Stacks,' the more I watched 'Les,' who was iced out in a diamond encrusted chain and a matching Cartier watch. I'd seen that 'get money watch' back when I was boosting, so I knew with all the extra diamonds, he'd spent about $20,000. Something didn't seem right. I just couldn't put my finger on it. I wondered what Samuel was doing mingling for so long with these guys, but as usual, I stayed in my place. One thing was certain, he wasn't selling no properties, or making a real-estate deal with these guys.

Things really seemed strange when Stacks called the waitress over to the table and pulled out a wad of hundreds.

He made some lavish request for all the ladies who either eyed him, or blew kisses from the bar. The first thing I thought was, *oh hell no...my man ain't gonna be rolling with these cats. I'd beat a bitch down trying steal my lotto ticket.*

But then it hit me. I didn't really know much about Samuel anyway. For all I knew, he could've been a mass murderer. He'd told me he was an entrepreneur when we first met. Then, he even showed me several houses he said he was renovating, giving me the impression that he was heavily into real estate. But hell, who knows.

"You wanna dance?" Les leaned over and asked me out of the blue.

I laughed a little at first, to see if Samuel was listening. I wasn't sure how he'd react.

"You laughing," Les remarked. "But you moving in your seat like you wanna get on the floor."

"Well...sure...I guess."

I stood up to scoot my way out of the booth, when the palm of Samuel's hand pushed me back down.

"What the fuck do you think you doing?"

"Uh...well...umm...your friend asked me..."

"Asked you what? What? You gon' let some nigga that you just met disrespect me right in front of my face!"

"Sam, I thought..."

"Shut the hell up."

My head snapped to catch the end of Les' laugh. He thought it was somehow funny.

"Man, don't blame her. I tried my hand."

I was truly confused. "Tried your hand?" I questioned.

"Yeah, stupid. This nigga is used to bidding on bitches we meet at the club. You my lady. That's why the fuck I'm about to fuck you up in here."

Tears welled up in my eyes, while embarrassment shot through my entire body. Samuel quickly stood up from his seat, and so did his shady associates. I didn't know if they were all standing for me or what, so I stood too.

Samuel could see that I needed a private moment, so he waved his hand toward the bathroom in a quick flicking motion. He wanted me gone from his sight! I moved fast with a rapid stride, hoping my tears wouldn't smear my make-up.

As soon as I hit the bathroom door, I let my emotions loose, and banged on the door of the first stall. I contemplated if that whole ordeal was my fault, or if Les was just tryna play me. I whipped my purse over to the wet sink and pulled out my cell phone. I needed somebody to talk to. Stacy's number was easy to remember, but when I heard that familiar whining sound, and the operator said the phone was unable to process, I knew at that moment, my cell service had been turned off. But of course…the bill hadn't been paid 'cause Essence was lying dead in an alley somewhere, or sitting at the bottom of a lake.

I jetted out the bathroom, ready to make amends and apologize to my man for disrespecting him, but when I got back to the table, no one was there. I searched the room and in between the crowds. Still no sign of Samuel. Apprehensively, I sat down and gulped down the only drink remaining on the table. I didn't care who it belonged to. Suddenly, I felt a pair of eyes watching me. Strangely, I knew it wasn't Samuel. My bald headed, white teeth stalker stood less than two feet away. He raised his glass, and checked his surroundings to see if the coast was clear.

I thought , *damn…please go away. Tonight is not the night.*

My stalker did just the opposite. He moved closer in my direction, leaned toward me, and flipped me an all black business card.

"Jerri is the name, sexy lady. I just need you to know the guy you're with is dangerous. If you ever need a shoulder to cry on, help leaving, or just someone to talk to, call me."

My mouth fell open as Jerri walked away and Samuel reappeared. Not sure if he saw Jerri talking to me, I rushed to crumble the card into the palm of my hand, and said a silent prayer. Lord knows I didn't wanna lose this good-looking man, or get beat down in the process.

Chapter Twelve

Weeks had gone by, and I found myself being bought like a cheap sale on Ebay. I'd gone from getting punched in the face on several occasions, to going with Samuel, *my abuser,* to the lot to pick out my new convertible six series BMW; then back to the house to serve out my prison term. *My baby could be so loveable, yet so psychotic.* I knew I looked good, but being locked up in the mini-mansion was a no-no. I needed to get out, strut my stuff, and take in all the sexual comments and whistles from men that made me feel like a woman.

I paced the kitchen floor in my full length cream colored silk robe, wishing the Absolute and cranberry juice would just disappear from my hand. It was near four o'clock in the morning, and the sun was gonna catch me soon.

As usual, my body behaved like a robot. It was so sad. Every night the routine was the same; I'd drink as many martinis as I could without letting Sam know I was near a drunken stupor. Then I'd wait until he'd fall asleep, only to hurry back downstairs and dress my drink the right way. Three olives on a pink toothpick, and touch of salt on the rim. Most say it doesn't blend, but damn, it sounds good to me even when I say it.

I stood by the sink, thinking about my life, my past, and my future. Not to mention Essence, and the fact that if anyone ever found out what happened, I'd get life. Besides, my conscious wearing on me, it seemed as though I was getting what I always wanted. A bitch had been searching for Captain-Save-A-Hoe for years, and now he was here. My only wish was simply for Samuel to lighten up a bit.

It seemed like the instant his name entered my mind, a ghost appeared. In the shadow of the darkness, Samuel stood ass-naked by the refrigerator rubbing his eyes. He looked so innocent, standing with his braids loose and damn near sweeping his waistline. He moved closer, with his dick swinging, hardening by the second.

"Why you up?" he asked softly.

"Just needed a drink. Guess I got a lot on my mind."

"You still mad at me?"

I hunched my shoulders, thinking back to our argument earlier in the day. "I mean…you been doing some foul shit lately," I said, in a low tone.

"Foul shit, huh? That's what you think?" His voice deepened.

I turned my back to him, not even wanting him to flip out.

"You didn't think killing Essence was foul?"

I broke down like a mother who'd lost her child. Leaning forward, I clutched my buckling knees. "You know I didn't mean to do that," I cried. "It was a mistake and you know it!"

"Oh…I didn't know you could slice somebody's neck by mistake. Think about it, Chanel. I put a lot on the line for you. I sent my boy, Lou into a dangerous situation that coulda got him locked up, just to save your ass. The moment you called me, I took care of it, didn't I?"

I screamed to the top of my lungs. "It wasn't on purpose!"

"Doesn't matter!" he shouted back. "If Lou hadn't gone over there and cleaned up your mess, and gotten rid of the body, you might be sitting in a fucking lil-ass jail cell right now, instead of a four thousand square foot house.

"That's fucked up, Samuel." I cried even more. "How long you gonna hold that shit over my head?"

"I'm not, baby," he said, moving a little closer. "I just need you to realize I'm here for you. I got your back always. Just like when I paid off the prosecutor in Detroit to drop those idiotic fraud charges."

My face squinted immediately. I never knew. How stupid could I have been. I just assumed the Good Lord was looking out for me. "I know you love me," I confessed, drying my tears. "I just wanna be happy in life, Samuel. That's all I've been looking for; happiness, and a good man to love me."

"That's what you got me for," Samuel replied, walking directly in front of my face.

The moment we stood face-to-face, it reminded me how similar we were in height. I laughed inside thinking, that's what made our sex so good. I wanted to look down to see if his stick was still expanding, but before I could say anything else, my head was forced backwards.

Samuel grabbed my hair, damn near pulling my weave out, and yanked my head back like I'd done something wrong. I knew it was foreplay. That's just how he got down, rough!

I was beyond ready, 'cause my shit was wetter than a soggy yard on a rainy afternoon. My head just tilted off to the side, while Samuel's tongue went to work all over my neck. He sucked, pulled, yanked and licked 'til I couldn't take no more.

I screamed, "Fuck me, baby!"

In an instant, Sam yanked off my robe, and commenced to sucking my Double D's. My body responded, and fell into a frenzy.

"Yeah, baby…yeah, baby." I scooted my body up and

down, while Samuel pushed me forcefully into the kitchen island. I started drooling out my damn mouth like a patient with cerebral palsy, the way he made me feel.

"Feels soooooo g-o-o-o-od. Damn!"

Samuel started making his sizzling noises, warning me that he was about to get crazy. That must've been some island shit, 'cause it sounded like a voo-doo call to me. Still in all, it didn't matter, 'cause I was about to get fucked right on my kitchen floor.

Next thing I knew, Samuel had somehow hauled my one hundred and sixty pound frame around in the air, gripping me by the ass, and slammed me forcefully onto the stove.

I looked back slightly, to see if he was about to set my ass on fire, then said , "Fuck it. It is what it is." I loved his kinky shit.

"Oh yeah, baby." I grinded, then gripped him by his butt cheeks, as he slid between my legs.

"Is this what you want?" He sizzled again. "S-s-s-s-zzzzzz."

"Yes…yes!" I yelled, trying to grab hold of his dick. I needed it. Wanted it!

He sizzled once again, but I stopped his moans with a nasty kiss. He took it for a second then moaned a bit. Soon as his crazy ass moaning was done, he dropped three inches down, and started licking me like a flavorful lollipop. I bucked like a horse going wild, ready to explode.

Samuel knew what he was doing. His tongue work was a masterpiece. I'm guessing a certified pro, 'cause he stopped, lifted me in the air, kissed me in the mouth, and dove back into his mid-morning meal.

He locked on my pussy so hard 'til it hurt. Then, before I could say ouch, his tongue began a gentle swirling motion that drove me wild; up and down, in and out, he flickered.

114

"Shit!" I hollered.

He ignored me, while making slurping sounds like he was sipping the bottom out of a 7-Eleven slurpie. He had me so gone, I couldn't hold back any longer. I bucked, then arched my back, screamed and hollered, while my juices splattered everywhere.

Samuel never moved. He stayed and cleaned the plate, while I screamed out my pleasure some more. In between my shouts, my eyes remained closed, so I never noticed when Samuel grabbed me by my legs and pulled me onto his dick.

Now he was doing the yelling. I thought that nigga was going through convulsions, so I took my shot at pussy whipping his ass. I pressed forward, and rode him with all my might. While he carried me slowly around the kitchen, I grinded up and down. Round and round, I fucked. Fucked like my life depended on it.

He started those crazy ass sounds and calling out my muthafuckin name. I knew I had him then. "Chaaaa-ne-ee-el!" he called, and tightened his grip.

I called out some shit too when he went deeper. Hell, deep as his dick could go, 'cause I felt every inch. That nigga was banging my insides out of position, but it felt good as a motherfucker.

Two seconds after our shouting match mellowed just a bit, Samuel flipped the script. His took his dick out rapidly, which had me ready to fight. Quickly, he turned me over, and had me in police position with my hands on the kitchen sink. He knew doggy-style wasn't my thing, and never put a smile on my face to say the least.

He gripped my big-ass and pulled it dead smack into his dick. Problem was he was going for the wrong hole.

"Hold the fuck up!" I shouted. "I thought we talked about the unforbidden hole."

"Come on, baby. When you said anal sex was off limits for you, I thought you meant them other niggas you used to fuck."

I shot him the look of death.

"I'm your man for life, baby."

"Umm...ump...I told you that don't give me pleasure no more. I had a bad experience."

He seemed pissed. "Turn back around then, before you make my shit soft."

I turned to face him, when he pushed my head with his left hand and inserted his dick where it belonged with the left. Instantly, we got back into our rhythm.

Samuel clutched my breast and dug deep into my big brown ass. My eyes rolled to the sides, while he stooped lower and got into that position which sent me into ecstasy. I hollered...he hollered...he moaned...I moaned. Then we spent next thirty seconds climaxing together.

Eventually, Samuel laid his head on my chest like his ability to breathe was a struggle. I continued to pant too, so together we looked like two dogs in need of a gallon of water.

"Damn, Chanel. That shit was right. You gonna have to come on your period or something, so a nigga can get a break."

Suddenly Samuel lifted his head and just glared at me.

"You okay?" I asked, then fixed my hair back into place. I needed to look good even after sex.

He nodded with three deep creases in his forehead. Whatever he was thinking was deep.

"When was the last time you had a period?" he asked.

"What?"

"A period. That's what. I just thought about it. We've been fucking for two months straight. I ain't seen no blood. Or even heard you talk about no blood. Nothing." He frowned once more. "You on that Depo shot shit?"

In a flash, I saw my world ending. I had to tell him.

No I couldn't. Then after a few seconds, I contemplated again. Time was running short. My man was staring me in the face. And I knew he would soon demand answers. I pressed my face into my palms.

"What is it, Chanel."

"Umm...Ahh...Umm..."

"What the hell is wrong with you? You gotta stop drinking so you can think clearly. Fuck this shit!" He moved slightly to the side, and lifted the empty glass off the counter.

"Oh, I'm thinking clearly."

"Then what is it?"

"I'm pregnant," I blurted out.

"Pregnant?"

"Yeah...p.g. with child." I smiled a little, then clutched my stomach while Samuel grabbed my thighs.

He kneeled to kiss my belly, then laid his head on my lap. "Damn, we having a baby."

"Um... hum," I said softly. My eyes instantly closed, while my hands commenced to rubbing his frizzy dreads; all along wondering why I opened my big mouth. But before I could harp on my mistake, another shock came my way.

"Marry me, Chanel."

"Huh?" I uttered.

"I said, will you marry me?"

Chapter Thirteen

I pranced in front of the smeared mirror, trying to steal one last peek at myself before taking the plunge. My off-white dress was skin tight, and fell just below the knee. I decided against a traditional dress, 'cause there was nothing traditional about me.

Of course, my hair was styled to perfection, but I had my faithful wire brush in my bag just in case a string moved out of place. My mother had always told me my special day was coming, and that I'd look great. It was just a shame she couldn't be here to share my happiness with me.

I had thought about calling her last week when Samuel proposed, but decided against it. It was too much for my family to handle, especially my brother. I figured I'd just show up in Detroit with a big rock on my finger, and they'd all forget about my past, and tell me how proud they were of me.

A loud bang on the door suddenly reminded me that my husband to be, and my only friend in ATL, were waiting on me on the other side of the bathroom door.

Stacy yelled, "Trust me, Chanel, you look good."

I grabbed my purse, and smiled into the mirror one last time. I was damn proud of myself. I'd gone from pillar to post, trying to find a man who'd marry me and take care of me forever. That day was finally here. If I could high-five myself, I damn sho nuff would.

"How do I look?" I asked, and did a twist for Stacy in the middle of the dusty tiled floor, as soon as the bathroom-door flew open.

Tears instantly welled up in her eyes. "You look so pretty."

I couldn't believe my friend was showing some emotion. "Girl, don't get all mushy on me and shit. You'll make my mascara run." We both laughed.

When we stepped into the miniature sized living room, Samuel was standing there in a custom made tan suit, looking so damn good, I wanted to just walk up and sneak a good rub on his crotch. He was sexy like that, and always got me moist even from afar. His friend, my savior, Jamaican Lou, stood near the mantle dusting like he really liked keeping his house clean. The place was a dump, and I was still kinda pissed that Samuel would even agree to have us married at his place. He knew how I felt about Lou, but for some reason, kept bringing up the fact that it was Lou who'd saved my ass from the Essence tragedy. He'd pleaded the night before about how Lou was also his best friend, and wanted to set up our nuptials. He'd gotten the pastor and everything. Somehow, Samuel couldn't refuse.

Lou stopped wiping dust for a moment, and stuck his hands into his pocket before examining me for the thirtieth time. He always seemed to glare into my face like he had a problem with me. I shot him back with that same defiant stare, and gave him the evil eye too.

"Fucka," I mumbled under my breath.

He never said too much to me anyway after the day I told him to fuck off. Samuel made the mistake of telling me that Lou said something wasn't right about me. So, from then on out, we just never clicked. *Hated him,* I thought.

"Are you nervous?" Stacy asked, causing me to take my eyes off of Lou.

"A little. Thanks for asking, girl."

I then walked toward my future husband and smiled.

"Lets do this."

"I couldn't agree with you more. You look beautiful as always, baby," Samuel responded. He went to grab my hand, but stopped when someone knocked on the front door. Then without even thinking, he turned around to see who it was.

"I'll get it, man. This my damn house. Relax," Lou joked.

While the fellas made their way to the door, I got all jittery inside. I stood up with my all white rose bouquet straddled between my hands, and started walking back toward the bathroom in a straight line like a princess at a royal wedding walking down the aisle.

Stacy followed me and laughed, "There's no need for all that diva walking and shit. We're gonna be the only ones here, so stop practicing."

"Oh, I'm gonna at least move some of that old-ass furniture in here and walk up to the mantle. Lou said that's where the pastor was gonna stand."

"Chanel, this is gonna be quick, just like going to the Justice of the Peace. The important thing is that you're getting what you said you always wanted, right?"

"Bitch, you always so damn philosophical. I'm getting Samuel, yes. But I wish like hell I coulda had a lavish wedding."

"You sure you wanna do this, right?" Stacy moved closer and put her hand on my shoulder. Her brows creased like she had some concerns.

"Absolutely."

"Just checking," she uttered, with a weird look.

I wanted to ask her what the fuck that crazy-ass look was supposed to mean, but when I heard the new voice coming from the living room, my heart stopped. Instantly, I walked back toward the living room and stood in complete shock as a man I never expected to see, walked up and shook

Lou's hand.

What the hell is he doing here, I thought. Then it all made sense once he asked Samuel for the marriage license. I got the glue face for a moment; couldn't talk, couldn't move. Nothing.

My body fell limp. It was hard to believe I was still standing. The chipped tooth and country style of dressing confirmed it was him. Pastor Scott turned to see me standing in the doorway to the living room biting my nails.

"This must be the beautiful bride?" he asked.

Pastor Scott held out his hand, yet my feet still wouldn't move. I just glared into thin air, wondering if he would continue to act as though we'd never met. I hadn't seen his ass since the night he was dressed in drag at Essence's house, and hoped that I never had to see him again, but I guess that was just wishful thinking.

Suddenly, Lou clapped his hands together loudly, sending the men into their places. As expected, my undercover lover turned backward, when no one was looking, to shoot me an evil eye. He walked up to the mantle, explained the quick process, and handled a little administrative work with his pen.

"We're all set," he announced, "Chanel, I'll need you and Stacy to stand here, and Samuel and Lou here."

For some reason, my body reacted like a robot. I moved as fast as I could, and popped into my space. Before I knew it, the wedding had begun. Pastor Scott had already said his initial words, but I'd fallen into a daze. With glassy eyes, I listened, but barely heard. Even when Samuel grabbed my hands and said his vows, I still barely processed his words.

"Ms. Martinez, repeat after me," Pastor Scott said.

I managed to cough up a smile and got myself together. "I, Chanel Martinez, take you, Samuel Blackmon, to have and to hold from this day forward, for better or for worse, for richer or for poorer, in sickness and in health, to love and to cherish from this day forward 'til death do us part."

As soon as I finished the last line, Pastor Scott gave me another evil eye, which immediately made me sweat. The hot flashes that were hitting my ass were far worse than the hormone issues I'd been fighting over the last few weeks. Samuel squeezed my hand, giving me the sign that he wanted to know if I was okay. My confirmation was simply a wide grin.

Before long it was all over, and I had a glistening three carat-emerald cut diamond on my finger. I looked down just as I heard the words, "*I now pronounce you man and wife.*" The way Pastor Scott put emphasis on the words *man and wife* was scary. No one else is the room noticed, but the way his voice fluctuated, told me he wasn't too happy about my nuptials.

Samuel took my mind away from it all when he closed in on me and sucked every bit of saliva I had out of my mouth. Our kiss was so passionate, it was sorta outta place. It was supposed to be a subtle kiss, not a slob down.

"Get a room," Stacy called out, as she started clapping.

Then, like clockwork Lou and Pastor Scott joined in the applause.

"Mr and Mrs. Blackmon," Lou shouted. "My man," he said to Samuel, followed by a strong hug. Of course I got nothing but a weak, "Congratulations."

"Thanks," I replied dryly. I wanted to say, *fuck you, Lou.*

Stacy, all of a sudden, pulled me with force. All her teeth were showing, so I knew she was happy for me. "Come with me, Mrs. Blackmon." She chuckled. "Sounds funny calling you that."

"Where are we going?"

"Right here in the kitchen," she pointed. "I just wanna

give you my gift. Let the fellas talk a bit," Stacy suggested, watching them huddle into a circle.

I needed to keep both eyes on that snake who'd just married me. Luckily, Lou's house wasn't bigger than two apartments put together, so Stacy and I would be only several yards away.

As soon as we stepped into the kitchen area, she whispered, "What's wrong with you?"

"What you mean? I'm fine."

"You look like shit. Your face is all flush. Something must be up, you've changed two shades of another color."

I looked over my shoulder to check on the fellas. Pastor Scott quickly cut his eyes my way. I turned away. I had to tell Stacy what was up. She was my best friend, so keeping secrets wasn't a good thing.

"Chanel, I'm worried about you." She folded her arms, and posed into a nasty stance, like she wanted answers. "You never told me what was up with the whole hospital ordeal. And I notice from time to time you're not feeling your best. And today…let's not go there, cause you look like the devil just touched you and won't let your ass go."

"I just need some water. I'll be fine." I tried to remember if I'd even taken my pills for the day.

"You been back to the doctor?" she edged.

"Yeah, I…"

I stopped mid sentence once I heard Samuel asking Lou for a pen so he could give Pastor Scott our number. It threw me for a serious loop. Stacy kept tugging on my shoulder, trying to get me to re-focus so her question could be answered, but I was stuck on stupid.

I moved two steps closer, to make sure I was hearing their entire conversation. By the time I'd gotten close enough, it was apparent that Samuel had given him our address too. What the fuck for, I couldn't figure out.

I looked behind momentarily, only to see Stacy on my heels. She looked confused, like something was really bothering her. Hell, we all needed to check ourselves into the nearest crazy house.

"We need to talk," Stacy sung into my ear.

I kept walking toward Pastor Scott. He needed to get told…exposed, right in front of everyone. "I'll tell you everything later," I said.

"Sure you don't wanna talk?"

"Nope," I answered strongly, just before reaching the huddle, where the men where exchanging goodbyes.

"Thank you so much for being here," I said to the man who used to act like a mute around me. My game face was on.

"Hey, we'll let Chanel walk you to the door, Joe," Lou said, as if he knew him outside of his religious role.

I thought, *Oh… ,so that's his first name*. But I wondered if it was his real name. I watched intensely, as my new husband patted him on the back.

"Hey, thanks again. I'll make sure I find you that property you're looking for. Just call me," Samuel said to him. He smiled at me, then looked back at Pastor Scott. "I've gotta make these final plans with Lou for this evening." He smiled at me again, like he had a hell of a surprise for me.

My new enemy and I moved closer to the door, chit chatting about the wedding, like I was so grateful for his services. As soon as I opened the door and walked out, I was prepared to blast his ass, but Samuel was standing in the kitchen doorway talking on his cell. He could see me clearly, and Stacy damn sho nuff was on police stakeout. You couldn't tell me the law wasn't paying her short ass.

"Thanks again," I said, reaching out to give Pastor Scott a hug.

"I know your secret," he whispered.

My jaw dropped low and my heart skipped a beat. I held my chest, while my temperature rose. I couldn't see my complexion, but I knew I had to be two steps from being purple. I needed to be clear about what he meant. Did he mean what happened with Essence? Or my serious secret? My life threatening secret?

"I'll be in touch," he stated with a snicker, before turning around. I clenched my jaw as he walked down the sidewalk, pimping like he was the man.

Chapter Fourteen

I crept through my neighborhood, driving twenty miles per hour. That was totally a disservice to my Beamer, but my eyes needed time to survey every block carefully. With one hand on the wheel, my neck swirled back and forth, making sure Samuel's car was nowhere in sight.

Even though we were still newlyweds and making love daily, he had to know there was something different about me. My disposition had changed. No more happy, lovee dovee shit. I barely focused long enough to carry on a normal conversation, and just laid there without any effort, when it was time for loving.

The worst part of it all was that I hadn't been taking my normal maintenance time for myself, or keeping my hair, feet, and nails done as usual. And I never seemed to sleep without sleeping pills. Ambien had become my new best friend. Samuel never said anything, but he was far from being a fool. If he'd seen me leaving the house with dry hair swept up into this wack ponytail, he would've known my mind wasn't right. I snapped from my pity party, and checked my rearview mirror one more time to make sure he wasn't following me.

For the past three weeks, I'd been sneaking out to meet Pastor Joe Scott and stayed on pins and needles. I thought about every word that exited my mouth, in hopes that I didn't trip up and reveal nothing. Hell, I was even afraid to go to sleep next to Samuel, praying I wouldn't talk in my sleep. Pastor Scott had me all messed up. When he revealed that he knew I had something to do with Essence's death, and that Lou and Sam helped me cover it up, he left me no choice but to see him. He just never made it clear what he really wanted from me.

The fact that he still wanted to have sex with me, after telling me my husband would kill him dead if he found out, was the craziest shit I'd ever heard. It seemed like it excited him. He did, however, make sure he strapped up each and every time.

When I pulled up to our meeting spot, I pushed my Christian Dior sunglasses closer to my face. They were jet black, and just what I needed to hide my pain. I had endured embarrassment all my life; always trying to be accepted, always trying to make others like me, or understand just who I really was, but I was tired. Marrying Samuel should've ended all of that, but Pastor Scott, or Joe, which is what I'd been forced to call him over the last few weeks, put a monkey wrench in all of that happiness.

I sat in the car, sulking and nervous as hell. When he drove up and parked beside me in his old white Infiniti Q45, my hands quivered just a bit. I knew it was his car, but the tinted windows got me a little shook. *What if the door opened and Samuel popped out? What if this was all a set up?*

The sound of the horn even scared me, but made me move a little faster. I gathered my purse and put my lockbox under the seat. A few minutes later, I was sitting in the front seat of Joe's musty smelling car.

"What's up, Chanel?"

"What's up, asshole…I mean Joe."

"That sarcastic mess just might get you in trouble," he suggested with a smirk, as he pulled off. "So, you been keeping my shit warm?"

I didn't respond.

"Now look, no need for attitudes while you with me. I

want the same Chanel that Sam gets. Understood."

I didn't respond again.

Out of the blue, Joe swerved the car over onto the median strip. "Now look, I'm in charge. When I ask you something, you speak...unless you want me to drive you home, so we can tell hubby all he needs to know about us. Understood?"

"Got it," I finally said.

Thank God he couldn't see my eyes. My glasses saved me from misery. I wondered what happened to the mute I used to fuck. All of a sudden he talked way more than before...too much.

"So, Sam got you on a tight leash, huh?"

"Not really."

"When I call him, you always seem to be home, waiting like a good little housewife."

I got upset instantly, but it was the perfect opportunity to get some answers. "Why are you calling my husband like he's your friend? He's not your fucking buddy."

"He's helping me purchase a property."

"And banging his wife is the perfect way to repay him, huh?"

"Are you really his wife?" he chuckled.

What the hell is that supposed to mean? I folded my arms, and breathed with the number ten in mind. I counted to myself one by one, hoping I wouldn't jump across the seat and whip out my razor. I believed in the Good Lord, and knew I'd go straight to hell for killing a pastor. But he deserved for something bad to happen to him. Payback was due, but I knew I had to be careful. He wasn't your ordinary pastor. As a matter of fact, I rarely heard him talk about church...and wondered if he even pastured a congregation. *Doubted it.*

"So, where we headed?"

"Our normal spot," he replied.

I breathed a heavy sigh.

"Oh, so you don't wanna go work on making a baby with me today?"

I blared over the music, "A baby? With you? Are you crazy or just stupid as hell?"

"Oh yeah that's right. Sam tells me you already having his baby," he said nonchalantly. He ended with a loud continuous laugh. He just wouldn't stop. It was crazed, sorta psychotic.

I couldn't laugh, but dropped tear after tear. I thought about jumping out the car onto the side of Highway 20. This man was truly gonna be the death of me.

I sat there sniffling, and trying to get myself together when I noticed a black Impala that crept three to four cars behind. I'd learned from Samuel over the last few months how to detect when we were being followed. It seemed to be happening a lot lately when I rode with Samuel. Only this time, I prayed it wasn't Samuel following me.

My eyes squinted as I studied the road hard, trying to get a closer look at the vehicle. My heart pounded, trying to make sure it wasn't my husband. Then it hit me, it was the same Impala that had followed Sam and I the week before. Now I was with the pastor, and the same Impala was on the chase. I sat up tall and paid close attention, 'cause this was serious.

"Hey, I know this sounds crazy, but that car back there," I pointed into the mirror, "It's probably following us."

Joe adjusted his rear-view mirror for a closer look. His expression told me that he was at least taking me serious. "Let's see if you're right, Miss Lady."

Joe picked up speed, dipped in and out of traffic, and took the Panola Road exit. Sure enough, the Impala followed.

"What did you do?" he asked, with two large crinkles

formed in his forehead. "Either the police are on to your ass or your husband!"

"I didn't do shit. I just know when I'm being followed. And it's not my husband," I said nervously. "Maybe it's someone from your congregation," I shot back.

He back slapped me quicker than I could turn my cheek. I flinched, then jumped clear across the seat and commenced to throwing punches. I'd had enough, and felt it was time to show Joe who I really was. We fought like Ike and Tina in the limo in the movie, 'What's Love Got to Do With It'.

Joe had to keep one hand on the wheel to keep the swerving car from crashing, while I got in some extra harsh hits. He probably never imagined I'd be so heavy- handed, 'cause I always carried myself so much like a lady, but I was tearing his ass up. It only took an extra second for me to make it all the way onto his lap.

I straddled him as best I could, and punched his country-ass all in his head. I wanted to knock his chipped tooth clear out of his mouth, but couldn't get enough elbow space for a wild swing.

By the time we made it to the top of the ramp, my glasses had fallen off, and I was still throwing punches like a certified boxer. My submissive state had disappeared. Things calmed down instantly when the Impala pulled up directly beside us.

In an instant, we both glanced directly at the car, praying we would survive the bullets. The driver smiled, lifted his hand, and held the black object in our direction. I froze and Joe obviously froze too. I wanted him to smash on the pedal, but we both just sat there with the look of a deer trapped in front of a speeding car. Horns blew from behind, yet we never moved.

When the driver of the Impala starting snapping shots,

it threw me for a loop. It took me a few seconds to react. As soon as my brain became functional, my hands tried to cover my entire face. I didn't know what was worse; being shot at, or Samuel getting copies of those photos. Me sitting on Joe's lap at the top of the ramp on Panola Road didn't look too good. My height made it look like we were on the seat fucking for sure. Besides, I didn't have my shades on anymore to shield at least my face from being directly seen. I would never be able to explain this one to my overly zealous husband.

The driver of the Impala snapped faster than the fucking paparazzi. The camera changed positions a few times, and the flash flickered, even though the sun hadn't completely gone down. Joe and I both tried our best to disconnect, but the driver had obviously gotten what he needed. Everything seemed to move in slow motion. Yet, he managed to pull off before us. I'm sure Joe probably thought this was all Samuel's ploy, while I assumed it was the police, maybe investigating me.

When my cell phone rang, I acted like a complete idiot. I dove into the passenger seat, and started throwing shit out of my purse onto the floor in search of my phone. It was a brand new phone that I'd just gotten from my husband, so I had to answer. The ring tone was loud and added to my nervousness. It was either Samuel or Stacy 'cause I didn't fuck with too many other people other than my hairdresser, and a few bitches I'd met at the salon I went to.

By the time I found it, I breathed a sigh of relief, but still had beads of sweat on my forehead. I answered while puffing out quick, short breaths, but then almost stop breathing when I heard my mothers voice. It was so good to hear from her after all this time.

"How did you get this number, Ma?" I asked softly.

"We looked in your brother's cell phone and got in

touch with your friend, Stacy, and she was kind enough to give me your number. I hope you don't mind."

My voice cracked a bit. I'm sure she could sense the worry in my voice. "No, not at all. I'm actually glad you called. How is Jerrell anyway?"

"Oh baby," she wailed, "I-I-I-I don't know how to say this." Her cries quickened and her words slurred a bit.

"What, Momma? What's wrong?"

"Your, your, your brother is dead!"

"What?" My voice deepened. Shock took over and I lost my train of thought. "Why? What happened?" I let my face fall into the palm of my right hand while I grieved.

I peeked over at the Joe, who didn't seem to have a care in the world. His eyes were completely on the road, while I sobbed like a baby. He never even asked or mouthed what was wrong. He just drove slowly, listening to my cries.

My brother and I were really close growing up, so the news hurt me deep to the core of my soul. "When did it happen?"

"Today," she informed. "You get a flight and come on home. You hear me?"

"I will, Momma. I will."

I hung up and boo-hooed like I was gonna die right there in the car. "My Jerell!" I screamed. Dozens of tears flowed before Joe finally seemed interested in my anguish. All my concerns about the mysterious Impala had taken a back seat.

"Who's Jerell?" he finally asked.

"My brother...he died today."

"Oh, sorry to hear that," he replied unsympathetically.

I gave him the *fuck you* look, and cried out even louder. He still didn't seem to care. *I guess it is what it is*.

Before long we'd arrived at the Hilton Garden Inn parking lot in Lithonia. I couldn't believe how insensitive this man was. Here I was with my eyes all puffy and bloodshot red, and he was acting like the day was gonna go on as usual.

"I can't do this today!" I shouted, as he pulled around to the side of the hotel.

He put the car in park, rolled down the window, and lit a cigar. His demeanor was calm and cool, despite all that we'd gone through on the way over. The gash on his forehead looked like it could've come from my ring, but hell, I didn't give a fuck.

"Let's get this straight. You will do this today," he puffed.

"No...I'm not," I said, in a lower tone.

"Don't get it twisted. I still call the shots," he boasted. "Room #122." He handed me the key. "Now stop crying, and go on in there and get fresh for Daddy. It's not negotiable."

I looked at him like I wanted to kill him. *That's it...that's what would have to be done*, I thought. I snatched the key, hopped out the car, and strutted toward the hotel room, sniffling and all.

Chapter Fifteen

I woke up the next morning, barely able to open my eyes. My tears had obviously dried up throughout the night, which stitched my lids tightly together and helped my fake eyelashes to fall off. Still in all, I could feel Samuels's grip around my body. We'd fallen asleep in the living room on the double wide sofa after I cried my heart out for hours. Samuel told me he couldn't relate, 'cause he was never really close to anybody in his family. But he consoled me all night, just as I expected him too. He was turning out to be a good husband, and I loved my life with him thus far. He had even lightened up a bit when I wanted to visit with Stacy.

"Hey beautiful," he said, rubbing my face in tiny circles with his thumb. "You feeling better today?"

"A little." I smiled slightly.

"Look here...I got an important call late last night from my uncle back in Jamaica. I got some family trouble myself."

"What kind?" I asked, with concern.

"Oh, don't worry about my fucked up family. You and your family are my only concern. I've already arranged for Stacy to travel with you to Detroit so you can be with your mother. I'll be there in time for the funeral." He kissed my cheek softly. "I just don't want you to be alone."

"I'd rather have you with me?" I told him between our intimate pecks.

"I know, baby, but this is really important. Otherwise,

you know I'd be on that flight with you today. I only need a day or so. I gotta get my uncle back here to ATL, fast, then I'll catch a flight out to Detroit. Okay?"

"Got it."

"That's my girl." He hit me on the ass, like he was happy about the plan. "I gotta shower and get going. My flight leaves at noon," he informed, raising from the couch. "Yours is at three. Stacy will pick you up. Got it?"

"Okay," I answered, feeling a little like I had no say in the matter.

Luckily, Stacy was my girl, and I genuinely thought she cared about me, 'cause going with me to Detroit to meet my family would be a mess. This wasn't a situation that I'd take just anybody into.

"Did Stacy say what time she'd be here," I yelled out to Samuel, as he reached the stairwell."

"Nah…just call her."

"By the way, baby. We gotta add your name to the deed on the house when we get back!" he yelled out.

"We sure do," I responded. "Yes," I shouted to myself, and did a little jig in place.

"As a matter of fact all my properties."

I hurried through the foyer to catch up with my husband. By the time I reached the bottom of the stairs, he was already at the top, looking down on me. "Sam…"

"Yeah," he responded, with his head leaning over the railing.

"Speaking of properties, did you ever find the pastor who married us a property?"

"Joe Scott? He's bullshitting. We talk a few times a week, but I'm not sure how serious he is. Besides, he needs a full fledged agent. I only have properties that I'm flipping just for investment purposes."

"Oh," I answered, with a dumb look on my face. "He's

weird. I mean does he even have a church?"

"Why you asking all these questions all of a sudden?"

"I just got the creeps when I was around him." I shrugged my shoulders. "Just something about him. I don't know."

"Honey, cool it. The man is indeed a good pastor of a well connected and respected church on the outskirts of Lawrenceville." He shot me a disapproving look. "I might add, he's a community leader, always in papers and stuff," he ended, walking away from the railing, as if to say, the conversation was over. "Oh, and Chanel," he yelled back.

"Yeah."

"Remember, you didn't like it when Lou said there was just something about you that didn't seem right." He laughed, just as I heard him shut our bedroom door.

I pranced back in the kitchen thinking about my plan to put an end to Pastor Joe Scott. Hell, I needed a drink!

***

Four hours later, I watched the front door like a hawk, waiting for Stacy to pull up. She told me not to be late, and not to bring a whole bunch of extra shit. I figured since I disobeyed her last request, I could at least be on time. I had three large Gucci rolling suitcases waiting by the door, along with an oversized duffel bag. There was no way my boots, my lace wigs or my many purses would fit into just the two bags allowed by the airline. Hell, I'd just have to pay extra. Compliments of Samuel, I had it like that.

When Stacy pulled up in her beat-up Nissan Altima, I swung open the door and hurried outside. We had plenty of time to make it to the airport, but the Atlanta traffic was tricky. In the middle of the day when you least expect, you could get caught in an unsuspecting traffic jam.

"You alright, baby girl?" Stacy asked, hopping out the

car, and rushing to wrap her arms around me.

"For now. Every time I imagine Jerell's face, I get choked up."

"Well, I'm here now, so you're gonna be straight." She smiled and grabbed one of the heavy suitcases on wheels.

As she turned to walk toward the car, I thought about the fact that Stacy was a true friend. Honestly, one I felt could be counted on no matter what. I started thinking about how Stacy needed to know the truth about me. Besides, my father knew and was so deranged, he might've ended up saying something anyway. She deserved to be told by me.

"Girl, what you got in here? A dead body?"

I laughed, locked the door, and dragged the other bags behind me.

Stacy ran over to help me. "You probably got a ton of make-up in one of these bags, don't you?" she joked. "Eye-lashes, blush, lip gloss, and all the shit that keeps you looking so good," she teased.

"You know it. A sistah gotta look good." We laughed together, and hopped inside Stacy's car.

On the way to the airport, Stacy tried to cheer me up. We talked about my days back in Detroit, my new life with Samuel, and how happy she was to find someone like me to share a friendship with. I loved her thoughtfulness, and told her that in Detroit not too many women had close relation-ships, 'cause it's a city of hateration. She laughed, and asked if that word was in the dictionary.

"Nope, not in the national one. But yes, in the city of Detroit, it's gotta be there."

Before long, we'd arrived, parked and had plenty of time to spare. We swung past a small eatery on Concourse C to grab a bite to eat. It had been killing me in the car to find a way to break the news to Stacy, but now was the perfect time. I figured I'd just blurt it out. Besides, if I told Stacy now, she could help me convince my family not to tell Samuel when he arrived in a few days.

We weren't even in our seats a good five minutes, before a waitress was at our table, rushing us like the place was packed.

"You got somewhere to go?" Stacy asked as she grabbed a menu.

The fast-paced waitress shook her head and flashed a fake smile, but we could tell she was still in a rush to take our order.

"Shit, just give us two orders of buffalo wings," Stacy barked. "And by the way maybe you should quit this job and go work for Nascar."

We both laughed when she had the nerve to roll her eyes. The moment the waitress left the table, I asked Stacy if our friendship was unconditional.

"Of course it is," she answered.

In my heart, I knew she meant it. I looked at Stacy, and felt good inside. For one, she liked me for me. She wasn't into borrowing my clothes, begging me for money, or borrowing my ride. I looked over at her button down cotton shirt and cheap looking capris, and thought, she definitely wasn't trying to be on no competition shit. She was really a true friend, through thick and thin.

I grabbed both of her hands and squeezed tightly, as she sat across from me, wondering what had gotten into me. She squeezed back, and we glared into each other's eyes. Stacy was still fine as hell, but my lust for her had diminished over the last few months. Good true friends were hard to come by.

"Stacy, I gotta come clean, girl…and be honest about some things.

"Shoot. I'm all ears."

"Well, you know when I was in the hospital I had a

few issues?"

"Yeah, I remember," she answered, becoming more serious.

"Well, I…"

"What? You know you can tell me."

"It's pretty serious."

"I figured that. But I need to know the details."

"Well…"

Once I finished telling Stacy the truth about me, she dropped my hands altogether, and looked like she wanted to grab some hand sanitizer from her purse.

"You know I figured something was up. That's why I kept asking you questions every time I got a chance. Especially after I read your mail that day," she confessed.

"Are you still gonna be cool with me?"

"You bet. I'll even go with you to the hospital when you get back to get a check up on that situation."

I never thought in a million years something so serious would be that easy to share. Stacy was actually the only one thus far who proved to be true to me, especially since she now knew my medical secret.

***

Who said traveling was supposed to be glamorous? It had been a long day, and a bitch like me was starting to get corns on my feet. I yawned and twitched in my seat while giving Stacy the last bit of directions. It wasn't too far from the airport, but the drive felt like an eternity. I'd bitten off half my nails, and sweated like a pig on the ride over.

A few minutes later, my body tensed up when we finally pulled the Chrysler rental car in front of my mother's house.

From the looks of things, nothing had changed. It was a small three-bedroom house on Harper Street on the east side of town. It reminded me of the houses in the movie, '*Boys 'N The Hood* ' except Crenshaw made my hood look like Beverly Hills. I knew I needed some quick maintenance. I flipped the visor down and pulled out my MAC make-up case. Within seconds, I powdered myself down, lip glossed myself to death, and transformed into a true diva.

I popped open the door, and stood outside the car for a few moments, unable to move. As my eyes scanned the neighborhood, it brought back memories; memories of Jerell and I riding our bikes down the street when we were young, and boxing as we grew older.

I was so uncertain about going inside. Between the loud babbling coming from inside the house, and the numerous cars that lined the street, I knew the house was full. I had no idea what to expect.

"Toughen up, and let's do this," Stacy remarked. She led the way, like she was now in charge.

We walked up on the steps and onto the wooden porch. When I opened the screen door, the entire room got quiet. I looked to my left at the long mirror trimmed in a gold outdated frame that still covered my mother's wall. My reflection caught my attention. *I look good*, I thought. But my skin tone had already changed a bit from the uneasiness.

My mother had seen me once since I'd gotten my new look, so she knew it was me. "C'mon in," she said to me.

I looked around the living room, thinking about how the house hadn't changed one bit. The same furniture, the same carpet, and the same pictures lined the long coffee table against the wall. I picked up the photo of Jerell and I, and got a little teary eyed.

My Aunt Charlotte saw me and asked my mom who I was.

"Who dat, Lillian?"

"It's Terell," she answered, looking downward.

143

I could tell she was ashamed of me. So I looked toward my aunt, so she could get a good look to verify that it was me.

"Terell?" she questioned. "Your son? My nephew? Jerell's twin? Oh, Lord!" she shouted. "I'm going in the other room to pray."

My drunk ass Uncle Walter was sitting on the couch with three yards of plastic wrapped around it, making tons of noises. "Uhmp, Uhmp, Uhmp… what is the world coming to."

I wanted to ask to borrow his flask. Instead, I walked over to hug my mother, and introduced Stacy. My voice was barely above a whisper, 'cause I didn't want the other people coming from the kitchen to see me at the moment. I had to handle each family member one at a time. I wasn't sure how many people were crowded back there, but it damn sho sounded like a basketball team.

The entire back room erupted with chitter chatter…I could almost imagine what they were saying about me. Both my Aunt Kyra and Uncle Paul, my father's siblings, peeped from the kitchen and sighed when they saw me.

My face was recognizable, I'm sure. I was shaped the same, same height, and same features. Only difference was that I'd gotten all my facial hair permanently removed and wore tons of make-up to make me look more like a lady. For years, they'd seen me transform into a woman, but I guess the long hair and sexy clothing was too much for them to handle.

My Aunt Charlotte came back down the steps, rattling on about God and the Bible, and how the way I was living my life was a disgrace.

"Aunt Charlotte, please don't start. Outta respect for my mother, let it go," I pleaded, putting my proper voice on. "Ain't nobody in here perfect! Nobody! I know all your little secrets too…you and you know who. So, don't think my shit stinks more than yours, cause it don't," I responded, with my hands on my hips.

"Baby, you's a transvestite too?" Uncle Walter asked Stacy, before taking another sip from his flask.

"No sir," she quickly responded.

I chimed in. "I'm not either. I'm a transgender. That's what you call it, idiot."

"Transgender? Uh…this is way too much!" my aunt shouted, placing her hand over her chest. "You mean you went all the way?"

"All the way," I said proudly.

"And she looks better than most models, doesn't she?" Stacy added, and tried to push me further across the room.

"Hell, she should. She's a tri-sexual!" my Uncle Walter shouted out with laughter.

"Transgender," I corrected. "Where in the hell were you when God was giving out brains?"

"In the wrong fucking line wit yo ass," he laughed crazily. "You was in the dick line, when you should've been in the pussy line." He started laughing so hard he fell over onto the old Jet magazines that lined the table.

I placed my hands on my hips, ready for war. I wasn't gonna be joked on at a time like this. I'd just lost my twin brother, and deserved the right to grieve just like everyone else. My mother knew me well, and could tell an explosion was on the way. Her words luckily saved my uncle.

"C'mon to the back, Terell. Your father should be home soon."

"Momma, it's Chanel. Call me Chanel," I pleaded, in an even lighter tone than I normally used.

She breathed heavily, like she couldn't bring herself to do it. "Okay…to the back, please," she responded.

As we made our way to the back of the house, all my peeping-tom-ass cousins, children of my Aunt Kyra and

Uncle Paul stared at me like they'd seen a ghost.

"Hey, Terell," they called, one by one.

I flicked them a fake wave. "Whats up?" I answered.

"How've you been?" my cousin Vicki asked.

"Fine," I replied, making sure to give her ass a one word answer.

It amazed me how much her facial features reminded me of Stacy. I wanted to ask her why she was still wearing multi-colored bad weaves this day and time. I had no time for her artificial bullshit, her or my other cousins. She could care less how I was really doing. She wanted to be flat out nosey.

They'd always tried to play me as we were growing up. They knew back then I had female tendencies, and made fun of me daily. But now I was, taller, stronger, crazier, and I'd whip they ass right in front of everyone if I had too.

"Hey, Terell," another one of my female cousins called out.

"Chanel," I finally shot back, and sat down in my mother's old lounge chair.

My mom pulled up a chair close to me, making sure her back was turned to the rest of the family. She told Stacy to make herself at home, and pointed to a chaise in the far left corner of the room. Stacy was tired, so she gladly plopped into the seat and got comfortable.

It felt good having my mom in my face talking to me like old times. I missed her so much. She'd aged gracefully. Pushing sixty-two, she still had a shapely figure, and a youthful spirit. Prayerfully I had her genes, and not my fathers.

We started off with an update on my life. She smiled slightly as I told her about Samuel, the wedding, our home, and all the positive news. Then we dove into how my brother actually passed. I cried a bit and she consoled me as she told me how prostate cancer had gotten the best of him. It was a disease that ran in my family, but for some reason, Jerell never stayed on top of his check-ups.

"We'll go by the funeral parlor tomorrow so you can see your brother alone. Okay?"

"I need that Momma. C'mere and give me another hug."

We embraced with a long hard clutch until I heard my father's voice in the front room. My mother jumped like King Kong had entered the building. She hopped up quickly and blotted her eyes with her wrist.

"I'm gonna go in the kitchen and fix you and Stacy a plate."

"Momma, I can handle him," I said to reassure her. I knew she was avoiding the situation. She didn't want my father to see her in an intimate loving setting with me. He wanted her to write me off just as he did.

I thought about my horrific past. Our horrific past. He'd caused me so much pain, yet I felt like the villain. Was I that bad in his eyes?

"Look," she pointed. "Despite our disagreements, I want us all to get along while you're here. Especially you and your father," she ended, with a smile.

"No problem."

The minute my mother walked away, my cousin Vicki interceded my space. "Chanel, I gotta know, girl…they said you went all the way. Did you?" Her voice was on volume ten, so it was all a set up. A clowning session if you asked me.

"I sure did," I said, with confidence.

"Your skin. It's so smooth. I mean, if I didn't know any better, I'd really think you were a girl.

"I am."

"Ahhh…yeah….sure you are," she smirked, and turned to look at my family members all watching and waiting.

"You see these jeans?" I asked standing tall. "You see

this ass?" I stuck my butt out as far as it would go. "Don't none of y'all tricks in here look this good. So, I am all woman!"

"Can you have children?" she asked, like she had one up on me.

"If you must know, I got the whole shebang done!"

"Shebang? What's that?"

"You know…the works…a pussy in all."

"But you still can't have children," Vicki smirked. "I watch the medical channels on cable. And '*Nip/Tuck*' too," she added.

"I can adopt," I shot back. "And I can afford to take care of them. What about you? Broke-ass!"

"What the fuck?" my uncle Walter shouted. "Where'd your dick go?"

"Yeah, where did it go?" Vicki chimed in, and folded her arms.

"Look, I'm about to start charging you. You asking too many questions," I told her bluntly.

"So, where's this invisible man who you claim loves you for you. I doubt if there's really anybody who would date you and wouldn't know."

"Oh, I got a man…as a matter of fact, a husband." I had one on 'em now. It tripped me out that the bitch Vicki had been listening to my conversation with my mother.

"But does he know?" Vicki asked with sarcasm.

"Yeah, does he know the hole you got used to be a dick?" Uncle Walter interjected.

"Fuck you, Uncle Walter. With yo drunk ass." I was ready to get every last one of them undercover tricks told. Then, I thought about the fact that Samuel would never be able to meet my family. If he showed up, they'd tell him for sure, and ruin my marriage.

Seeing that I was under attack, I gave 'em all something to talk about for days and my ass to kiss while I talked shit. "Yeah, in Brazil honey, they do the whole damn thing; the transgender operation, titties, butt injections…everything. Cost me over $100,000 to look this fabulous…and my man paid for it all," I lied.

"Terell, you will not stand in here and disrespect my house," my father announced, in his baritone voice.

A lump formed in my throat as soon as he made himself visible. He was still a heavy-set man, and with his height, he towered over most of us in the room. I wanted to cry, but I had to stay strong. He'd aged more than I expected, probably from the drinking. Yet, his skin still reminded me of a Cherokee Indian, and resembled my skin texture in many ways.

"You need to get your son straight!" my Aunt Charlotte shouted. "This is terrible. You already lost one son."

"All of you need to shut up and mind your own damn business! This is my life, my body!" I shouted.

"Either you go and take off all that girlie girl crap, or leave my damn house," my father announced, in front of everyone.

I thought about telling everyone why I probably turned out wanting to be a transgender Then, I looked into the kitchen, to see my mother leaning on the counter with tears streaming from her eyes. She was too afraid to speak up, and I loved her too much to have her in the middle. I gathered my things, and told Stacy we needed to leave. We said our goodbyes and pretended as if we'd see everyone at the funeral. I knew I wasn't staying in Detroit for long. I figured I needed to get back anyway to finish my plot to destroy the pastor. I just needed to call Samuel to tell not to even head this way.

***

"Unfuckin believable!" I yelled out to Stacy, while we were headed back to the airport to grab a hotel for the night.

149

"A few hours in town, and I've already fallen out with my family. We're on the first thing smoking," I said sadly. I was trying to be strong, but thoughts of my twin brother infiltrated my mind.

"I didn't even get to see his body, Stacy," I cried.

"Oh…we can fix that. Let's swing by the funeral home in the morning. I'm sure because you're the brother….I mean sister, you'll be able to see him."

"Thanks, girl."

"You bet," she replied, with concern.

"Stacy? Do you think differently of me now?"

"Hell nah." She smiled. "You still my girl. Even more so now…cause you told me the truth. But you know I got some deep questions for your ass later," she joked. "Starting with where the hell did the pipe go?"

I answered just like Miss Celie in '*The Color Purple*, "Inside of me."

Stacy laughed. "Damn all that meat gone to waste."

Chapter Sixteen

The sight of the Georgia Dome made me smile on the descent into the Hartsfield-Jackson Airport. The flight had gone smoothly for the most part, until our rookie pilot hit the runway like he'd just downed a forty and smoked a fat-ass blunt. ATL may have been new to my system, but it was now what I called home. It sorta grew on me, rain and all. Besides, Detroit had given me multiple headaches and now left a bad taste in my mouth.

After Stacy and I landed, we strutted toward the Baggage Claim, swinging our arms like we were near exhaustion. Stacy talked, while my mind flipped back and forth to images of my brother lying in that casket. I smiled slightly, thinking, at least I'd gotten one last opportunity to see him before his burial. However, I was still upset at the fact that my presence at the funeral wouldn't be missed.

"Girl, stop daydreaming," Stacy said to me, just after I bumped some little old lady with my Louie Vuitton cosmetic case, which I always carried with me on flights.

"Girl, a bitch is tired. Can't you tell? I'm all glassy-eyed and shit."

"You'll be okay. When I drop you off at home, just get some rest. Is Samuel back yet?"

"I think so," I responded, checking out my Presidential Rolex. Even the new diamond bezel Samuel had purchased for me a week ago couldn't make me happy. "His flight was supposed to get in either two hours ago, or two hours from now. Girl, I can't remember. Too tired, and too much shit on my mind," I snickered, waving my hand with frustration.

"Do you think he's curious as to why you told him not to come to Detroit?" Stacy questioned.

I let out a heavy sigh. "Probably so, and I know his ass is gonna have a ton of damn questions, so I gotta get my story straight."

"Look, Chanel, don't let all that confusion back at your parent's house get to you. You're a good girl. You got a good heart, and good things will happen to you. Don't forget that."

Stacy placed her hand just above my waist to console me as we stepped onto the escalators. Her demeanor warmed me. It was almost as if she knew just what to say to calm my nerves. We did, however, look a little strange together. Her little short behind consoling my tall ass earned us a lot of weird looks. But you know I didn't give a fuck. With all the chaos on my brain, I was liable to go postal anyway. *Let a motherfucker say something to me, or even look at me wrong*, I thought. I'd be ready to kick off my heels and get down and dirty.

"Now, let's just hope it doesn't take forever for these bags to come around the conveyor belt," Stacy said, the moment Baggage Claim was in sight.

"How 'bout I sit over here," I said, pointing to a seat near the door. "Give this twenty dollar bill to that funny looking sky cap over there. I just can't do any lifting, thinking or nothing. I'm drained," I ended, walking toward the hard seat near the exit doors.

I dropped my body down in the seat, like I'd worked the midnight shift at some warehouse lifting fifty pound boxes. Stacy kept turning around, watching me from afar, I guess making sure I didn't roll to the bathroom to perhaps slit my wrist. Shiiiit, I surely needed to be watched after what I'd gone through. My head thumped just wondering how I'd cover up my mini-depression from Samuel, and how he'd never be able to meet my family.

I sat pleasantly uninterrupted just staring into thin air. All kinds of what ifs and whys played tricks with my mind. Suddenly, anxiety took over. I twitched in my seat several times, until the first tear actually fell.

I hopped up and paced the floor like something had just happened. It didn't take Stacy long to notice that something wasn't right. She came running like my savior, hopping in front of the sky cap who toted our luggage and a large dolly.

She did her normal comforting routine, and talked to me like a psychiatric patient for a few moments. Then instructed me to wait curbside until she pulled the car around. I looked at the sky cap, who reminded me Arsenio Hall with his big-ass grill. I did just as I was told. I flicked my hand, motioning him to follow me with the luggage, and bit my nails down to the cuticles, waiting for Stacy to pull around.

Before long, Stacy had scooped me, the luggage, and gotten a number from some sexy white guy who helped us load the car, even though we already had help. I didn't do shit, couldn't even lift a finger to help. My body just plopped into the seat as my migraine intensified.

The entire ride home, Stacy chit chatted like I was really listening to her. She took a slight breather when I told her I needed some water, and quick, 'cause I'd forgotten to take my countless prescriptions, especially my hormone pills. At least now I didn't have to hide my medication anymore.

I ran down my list of meds for Stacy, and what each pill did for me to help solidify my transition into womanhood. The more she talked and questioned me, the more my head pounded. Finally, she pulled into the Chevron gas station off Old National Highway in College Park.

"Just water?" she asked, pulling into the station.

"Yeah. I can get it though."

"No. Stay here. You're a little suicidal right now."

"Get the damn water!" I yelled out. "No time for games."

I threw my heavy hand up against my forehead and sighed. I leaned back and thought about closing my eyes for a quick second, but just didn't feel comfortable. The cream colored Ford that sat across the street with its headlights on suddenly caught my attention. The sun had already begun to set, so seeing inside the car made it difficult. Two bodies seemed to occupy the car, but the more my eyes zoomed in for a better look, the more the car inched away from my view.

I sat straight up with concern. I was sick and tired of being watched. Something just wasn't right. Samuel had already preached to me about watching my back. He said thirsty thugs were constantly lurking the streets, trying to rob any and everybody that even looked like they had a couple of dollars. I figured if the car came too close, I'd have to figure out my plan.

I instantly reached for the horn, and then looked inside to check on Stacy, when I noticed her in line at the counter. I wanted to warn my friend in case the car rolled up on her as she came out the door. But before I could blow the horn to get her attention, three undercover cars, and two Dekalb County police cars rolled up into the gas station like the militia. The sirens were loud and bright, drowning out any music that played inside opened car doors.

The colored strobe lights and all the officers with DEA jackets written across the back had me jilted for a moment. They all jumped out surrounding the car and looking like I was some type of serial killer. *Oh shit!* I thought. *What if this is about Essence? What else could it be?*

It didn't take long for me to recognize the round-shaped gentleman with two separate stomachs hanging over his pants. He quickly stepped from the same cream colored

Ford that had just stalked me from across the street. His car was completely blocking Stacy's, so even if I wanted to pull a damn Thelma and Louise move, I couldn't.

He walked slowly, as if his breathing troubled him, while I sat frozen in awe, wondering once again what the hell this was all about. From the corner of my eye, I saw Stacy run out from the store, only to be stopped by one of the officers in uniform. The agents and officers had the whole gas station on lock, daring anybody to make a wrong move.

Suddenly, another officer, slightly younger than fat-so, pranced toward me with a confident swagger, and with his hand draped across his pistol. After eyeing him a few seconds, I realized that he looked very familiar, like I'd seen him somewhere before. He wore dark blue pants, a tightly fitted t-shirt, and had a wide grin on his face, as the older officer spoke. His pearly white teeth would've been the perfect addition to a fucking Crest commercial.

"Terell Martinez, we're gonna need you to come with us to DEA headquarters."

The younger agent had his eyes fixed on me so hard, I couldn't focus on the speaker. His tongue hung from his mouth like a salivating dog. On one hand, he'd heard the other agent call me by my birth name, but he stared at me like he wanted to fuck anyway.

"Terell? Who's that?" I asked, with the straightest face I could muster.

I scrambled in my purse looking for some identification. *Okay, maybe this isn't about Essence. They know my real name. I know Samuel paid off the prosecutor for that credit card fraud shit. Maybe it has something to do with that.*

"Sir…Miss, put your hands on the dash," the bald-headed younger officer said firmly. "Step out of the car with your hands behind your head." His hand straddled his holster, and his expression told me he meant business.

156

I was humiliated. Slowly, I stepped from the vehicle as instructed like I'd just robbed the convenience store. I turned to check my surroundings, 'cause a bitch was ready to go off. I just wanted to see if the bystanders who were starting to gather around had their camera phones ready.

Stacy was still being restrained by an off-brand officer in uniform, but that didn't keep her from talking shit. "She didn't do nothing!" she shouted. "Why you fucking with her? That's harassment! Ass holes!"

My body started to tremble. "What's this all about?" I interrupted, trying to take the attention off of Stacy. Then it hit me. "Wait a minute…D.E.A. Doesn't that stand for Drug Enforcement Agency?" I questioned, then continued without waiting for an answer. "I don't sell nor do drugs, so what do want with me?"

"Miss, we're trying to handle this the right way," the older agent said calmly. "No handcuffs, nothing harsh. Just come with us. I'm Agent Kofee, and here's my badge." He flashed that silver plated shit like it made him official, then placed it inside his triple XXX sized pants.

I glared at him, wondering if he could be trusted. It was almost as if he knew what I was asking. He shot me a look of sympathy. "Just come down for some questioning. That's it." He opened his hand and swayed it toward the car. The invitation was clear.

I looked at the younger agent, who appeared to be irritated by the no handcuffs suggestion even though he didn't say anything.

I decided to give in. "No handcuffs?"

"No handcuffs," Agent Kofee confirmed. "Have your friend follow us downtown, or you can call her when you're done."

I followed Kofee to the back of the Ford where he forced my hands from my head and down to my side. "Get in," he ordered, just before shutting the door.

My motorcade instantly started to break up as all the officers zoomed out the lot and headed their separate ways. I turned back slightly to catch a glimpse of the road behind me, hoping Stacy was following, but didn't see her car anywhere in sight.

At first Kofee drove in silence, as he munched on a king-sized snickers bar. Soon enough, I heard the wrapper making crumbling noises and his questions began.

"So, you got yourself into a little mess, huh?"

"Not sure what you mean," I responded, with sarcasm. "I'm just trying to figure out why I'm in the back of a police car…and on my way to be questioned."

"Oh, come on, don't play dumb…you know why."

"What? I don't," I snapped. "Maybe you should tell me."

"So, you mean to tell me you had no idea that your husband is a drug dealer. A Kingpin at that!"

"What? That's not true," I snapped.

He nodded his head back and forth, as if to say I was a great liar, or just plain stupid. "You willing to say that on the stand? Because believe me lady, you might have to. Conspiracy is a hell of a charge."

I freaked out. "Conspiracy to do what? I haven't done anything. And don't believe my husband has either."

"So, you're telling me you really didn't know?" he asked, adjusting his rearview mirror to see if my facial expression appeared to be truthful.

I folded my arms across my chest, and looked the other way. I guess a part of me felt stupid. I was never clear on what Samuel did. It was all too shady, any way you looked at it. But I guess finally having a man to love me, I just overlooked what he could've been into.

"You know we've been following you for weeks,

right?"

I shook my head up and down, not to appear overly
naïve.

"Does your so called husband know that we have pictures of you riding some man's dick in the car?"

I was speechless. *So, these assholes were the people in
the Impala. Damn.*

"And… we've been following your husband for over
six months."

I still offered no words.

"Look, I'm just trying to talk to you, and show you
some respect. Trust me, when we get into the station, all nice-
ness will cease. The rookie agents on your case will be
rough."

"It is what it is," I whispered softly, and continued to
glare out the window. I had to appear strong, even though
mentally I was weak as a lamb.

Before long, we'd arrived at the station near Centen-
nial Olympic Park. The street lights were on, but seemed to
be dimmer than most. Kofee pulled through a gate in the back
of the station, and drove directly up to a back door that had a
large keypad. He parked quickly, hopped out, and opened the
door for me. The moment I stepped out, a tall Herman the
Monster looking man in his thirties met us at the door. His
frown made me cringe, and his wondering eyeball in his left
eye put fear in my heart.

Instantly, he whipped out his cuffs. "Hands behind
your back."

I looked to Kofee for help, instead he turned away and
headed up the long cemented hallway. We followed suit, me
trailing like an inmate until we made it to the end of the hall,
where one stairwell led us down a flight of stairs and into an
office near the back of the building. It resembled one of those
interrogation rooms that I'd only seen from watching, *The*

Wire.

The room felt dreary, and it all became so scary, especially since Kofee had disappeared. I sat biting my nails as the Herman the Monster look-a-like paced the floor, and flipped through some papers inside a manila folder.

"Can you loosen the cuffs, they're kinda tight," I winced. I leaned forward and squirmed in my seat acting like this was a serious problem.

"You might as well get use to 'em, Terell, Chanel, or whoever the fuck you are. Where you're going, cuffs will be a part of your wardrobe. The beauty of it all, is finding out what dorm you'll be in."

I expected the murky-looking cock sucker to laugh since, he thought it was all so funny, but he maintained his frown. Clearly, he was ready to charge me, and I hadn't done a thing.

"Let's cut to the chase. Sign this. I've already signed under my name."

I looked down at the paper and read his name clearly…Agent Caldwell. My problem was understanding why Agent Caldwell thought I was gonna sign and confess to the lies on the paper. I wasn't confessing to shit.

Before I knew it, Caldwell had a tight grip under my neck, and was putting full pressure down on me. Tears welled up in my eyes. I wanted to fight back. I just couldn't bring my body to react.

"Your hubby is next door telling investigators that you were a co-conspirator," he announced, letting go of his grip. "His ass is already going up north. Your fate just depends on if you wanna cooperate."

"I said I didn't do nothing! You can't keep me here!" I shouted. "I know my damn rights."

"Your husband is a money maker. You know that, right?" He shook his head with pity. "But we got his ass. And got 'em good. Yep," the agent smirked, like Samuel's capture was his personal victory. "We got his ass on money laundering, conspiracy, and murder!"

"He is not a murder!" I shouted. "Lies, lies, lies! I need to call my lawyer!"

Suddenly, the younger agent from the convenience store walked into the room and right up to my face. Despite the fact that he was an asshole, he was fine as hell, and the old school Joop cologne he wore smelt wonderful.

"You should've taken my advice at the club that night," the younger agent said, showing his perfect white teeth again. "I told you the guy you were with was dangerous."

It was at that moment, when I realized the younger agent was Jerri from Club Platinum, and the guy who'd handed me his business card that night. *Damn, those bastards have been watching us for a while*, I thought.

"Since you wanna call your lawyer, you wanna call your husband too?" Agent Caldwell laughed, for the first time since he'd been in my presence.

"I thought he was next door," I snapped. My eyes rolled as if I had one up on him.

"He slid my metal chair across the floor making a loud irritating skidding sound. "I gotta make you a believer," he commented, as he slid open a large sliding window which exposed a double-sided glass.

My eyeballs nearly popped out of my head, as I watched my baby get yelled at and interrogated by two angry looking agents. Samuel looked like he'd been beaten, and his eyes seem to droop like he'd been there for a while.

"Samuel!" I screamed out, leaping from my seat.

"Oh…so you want him to hear you?" Caldwell asked.

I want him to know I'm with him…and not against him. I'm not signing shit," I spat, looking at the paper on the metal table. I sat back down, trying to read lips and make out

161

the conversation through the glass window.

"Your husband has moved more drugs across the Jamaican borders to the U.S. than you could ever imagine. And you helped him," the younger agent said.

I jumped from my seat again, only this time, my left jaw got met with a hard punch by Caldwell.

"No, I didn't," I grunted softly, while clutching my face.

"Now sign," Caldwell said, grabbing my arm and pushing me back into the table. The next thing I knew, he was waving a cheap ballpoint pen in my face.

"I know what we need," Caldwell teased. "A little phone call."

I glanced back over at Samuel, wishing I could hear his conversation. I knew he hadn't implicated me in his mess. I just knew it.

Agent Caldwell spoke into the phone. "Yeah, turn it on. Let them hear. Go ahead…tell 'em." he repeated. He grinned wickedly into my face.

"Let's see what he thinks about you being a damn man."

Before I could scream, "Noooooooooo!" Samuel turned with a solemn grimace on his face, and glared like he was having a stroke.

He moved closer toward the double-sided window, as the officers with him mouthed something I couldn't make out. The closer he got, my heart pounded. I was almost ninety percent positive they'd told him I was on the other side of the mirror. His face showed defeat. Mine showed fear.

Chills spread through my body. I placed my hands against the glass, praying he'd do the same. I was willing to go down with my man. I just needed him to believe in me, or at least hear me out.

"Chanel, tell me you're not in there, and the shit

they're saying isn't true," he mouthed, with his hands and face pressed against the glass.

I barely heard him, but realized from Caldwell's new phone conversation that the sound could be turned up even more. The officers decided who, when and where we'd all be heard.

"This shit can't be true!" he shouted. "Aaaaagggh-hhh…..noooooooo! You're my fuckin wife! You married me! You're pregnant, right?"

His emotions were spiraling out of control. I began to cry, thinking about what I had done. I loved my man. Why didn't I ever tell him? I could hear all of the agents laughing.

"They're trying to turn me against you, baby," I uttered.

Samuel shoved his hands in between his dreads and twirled his body around the room. I wasn't sure if he was crying, thinking, or preparing a plan for my death.

Finally he raised his head. "Terell!" he shouted, "I married someone named fuckin' Terell!"

I cried out loud, knowing it was over. My life. My dreams. My future. All over!

"At this point we're gonna let you go," the agent said from behind me. "When you're ready to come back and testify for us, let us know. I'm sure your hubby won't be so receptive as to having you back. Where will you go?" he questioned. "Might as well keep him off the street. Might save your life." He winked.

I hurried toward the door as soon as Agent Caldwell opened it. Unfortunately, I was met with my worst fear…my husband. He was being led in handcuffs from the room next to me, surrounded by three officers. They all had wide smiles while Samuel wore a face of embarrassment. His mouth said nothing, but his terrifying facial expression said it all. Samuel was big on respect, and this was considered disrespect to the tenth power.

"I'm sorry, Sam!" I yelled out. "I should've told you."

Wrinkles formed in the creases of his forehead. "What did you do, Chanel? I'm not crazy! I was inside you! And you told me you were pregnant! "

"I know, baby…I know…" I continued, as they pushed him along. "I got the surgery," I tried to explain. "I'm a real woman, believe it or not."

"You got tits…ass…tell me this shit is a joke, Chanel." He paused and looked toward the agent, who was shoving my file in his face.

"I've had enough of this romance shit. Here's the truth." Agent Caldwell shoved several papers in front of Samuel's face. One, my birth certificate. Two, pictures of me growing up, and three, a copy of my first drivers license.

I tried to throw his attention off. "Baby, I'll get you outta here. Then we'll discuss it all. I'll make it right. I promise. "

"Check in at the arraignment in the morning," Kofee announced, from the end of the hallway.

Boy was I glad to see him. "What time?" I quickly asked.

"No need," Samuel interjected.

Suddenly, Samuel yanked away slightly from the officer. His body jerked toward me like he wanted to knock my ass out. I flinched and swung my head to the left, hoping he wasn't really trying to hit me. Quickly, the officer yanked him into place, so they could proceed down the corridor.

Obviously Samuel didn't need to see any more photos, documents, or hear any more words; especially from me. He shot me the same evil look he'd portrayed when someone upset him while handling business. I figured he'd say all that same nasty, threatening shit I'd heard him say to his associates on the phone many times before. I just never thought I'd be walking in their shoes. It also hit me that since I'd learned the truth about Samuel, he could also have a bounty out for my head the moment he got a hold of a phone, or posted bail! I'd earned a death sentence tonight, and the only thing I could think about was how to explain myself to my husband.

By the time the DEA agents let me go, I walked out of the station like a zombie and with nowhere to go. I thought about who I'd call, until I got to the bottom of the staircase, and spotted my old trusted friend Stacy, sitting right out front in her raggedy Altima, tapping the steering wheel. She had a patient expression that told me she wasn't going nowhere.

I hopped in and breathed a sigh of relief. "I can't believe you waited for me. Thanks for being here."

"Girl, you know I wasn't gonna let you rot in no jail cell," she joked. "But what was that shit all about anyway? I kept calling, and they said you wasn't gonna get locked up...that you was just down here for questioning. What the fuck is up?"

"My grave."

"What are you talking about, Chanel?"

I sat back in the seat. "Well, for starters, my husband is a big time drug dealer and has a team of enforcers who've killed for him." I took the deepest breath possible before breaking the news. "And now he knows I was once a man. So, I'm good as dead."

Stacy's jaw dropped as far as it could go. She started the engine and pulled off slowly, with a fearful look on her face. "So, where we going?"

"Hell if I know," I responded, as my heart skipped another beat.

Chapter Seventeen

Stacy and I cruised all over Atlanta, unsure about where to lay our heads. The silence in the car amazed me. Neither of us knew what to say or think, which was rare. Most times, I'd always have some slick comment to make, or some cheap words ready when I wanted to bash somebody's character. Not tonight! My soul was stagnant and fear ruled the car.

We'd used up a half a tank of gas, and had less than a quarter remaining. But just the thought of Samuel being arraigned the next morning had me so much on edge that gas was not an option. Stacy's house was out of the question and mine was certainly a no-no, so I instructed her to just keep her foot on the pedal. Hell, I didn't even wanna stop at red lights. So for me, whatever gas we had was what we were stuck with for now. I was like a hoe running away from her pimp, so even parking where Samuel would potentially find me became an issue.

When we rode pass the Martin Luther King Memorial on Auburn Avenue, it made me wonder why I'd never chosen to explore Atlanta a little more before. This was an important landmark and it took me being on the run to head this way. *My mother would be so disappointed in me*, I thought, with disgust.

All she wanted for me was to have a good, stable life. One with no drugs, violence, and certainly not a drastic change in my life that would carry so many emotions. I breathed heavily and looked at the digital clock on Stacy's dash. It was nearly midnight, and we didn't have a clue what was next.

"What about a hotel? There's too many in the city for Samuel to find us, especially if we go out to Duluth or something," Stacy finally said.

"Stacy, please just keep driving, 'cause I don't know what Samuel is capable of."

"Chanel, I know you don't wanna hear this again, but I told you this is the only time you'll be able to get your stuff out of Samuel's house. From what you've described…let's face it. He may not want you back. And he might want you dead."

I didn't speak. My arms were folded, as I shook my head from side to side like a crazed woman. A tiny part of me believed Samuel and I could work this out.

"You hear me? This is your last chance! Your clothes, your car, everything is there! Besides, you can't live off that damn two hundred dollars in your purse!"

I continued shaking my head, as the tears flowed like Niagara Falls.
My mascara smeared the more I wiped away my puddles of sorrow. Nothing could spare me. I'd fucked up for sure. Strangely, I began to feel numb, and just closed my eyes as we passed the famous Atlanta UnderGround to keep from passing out.

Thirty-five minutes later, I had finally given in and sat parked out front of my house like a robber on stake-out. It was a little after 1 a.m., so barely a sole was in sight. If my neighbors even caught a glimpse of me looking like an unknown homeless woman, they'd immediately call the cops.

I clearly didn't look like myself. My weave was matted, and not a curl was in sight. My makeup mixed with a combination of tears, had smeared all across my face. I'd even kicked off my heels and chosen to go barefoot across the lawn, headed to the front door.

"Don't forget," Stacy whispered from behind, "make it quick. We'll only get the important stuff. And definitely get the car. We'll stash it in my cousin's garage. He lives in Conyers."

"Yeah, yeah, yeah. I heard you," I responded, with frustration.

I knew Stacy was right. At least my car was paid for. I could sell it if I got hard up for cash, which seemed to be likely in the near future. But reality just wasn't something I wanted to face at the moment.

When I stuck my key in the knob and opened the door, my emotions flared. The house seemed spooky for some reason. Maybe because I knew Samuel wouldn't want me here anymore. I quickly sucked my emotions back in, and ran toward the staircase. My sized twelve and a half feet took the stairs two at a time, while Stacy hollered from below.

"I'm coming right up. I'ma check the house for some cash. If he was doing all they say, he gotta have some money around here somewhere."

"Sure thing," I said, contemplating on going straight to the place where I figured the money would be. If there was any, it would be locked in his personal room. But it didn't take long for me to come to my senses. I dismissed the idea, and jetted toward our bedroom instead.

Once inside, it didn't take long to realize that the house had already been ransacked. Clothes were all over the floor, the mattress was turned over, and every picture that lined the wall had been broken. The DEA obviously had a field day looking for evidence to build their case. Trying not to let that slow me down, I ran over to my walk-in closet, and stuffed my best dresses, and favorite items into my faithful Louie duffel bags. This seemed all too familiar, and becoming the story of my life; packing my bags and moving on. I was almost sure my life with Samuel was on the road to being permanent. And now this shit.

"Girl, what the hell is taking you so long?" Stacy asked, as she bum rushed her way into the room.

My neck swirled around. "I'm moving as fast as I can," I snapped, dropping to the floor to pull my favorite heels from beneath the bed.

I looked over at Stacy, who'd gotten with the program, instead of talking me to death. She moved much faster than me, and had two bags fully packed in no time.

"I'm taking these down, and I'll meet you downstairs. Hurry, Chanel!"

"I'm coming, damn it!" I never even looked up.

When Stacy rolled out the door, I kept looking around the room unsure about what I was really searching for. I really didn't want to leave, but I knew I had to go.

I dragged my suitcase out the room on its wobbly wheels, and headed toward the steps. Suddenly, my eyebrows creased. The forbidden room had my undivided attention. It amazed me how Samuel never wanted me to go inside. Why, I always wondered. I guess love, or shall I call it stupidity, always kept me out. Not anymore!

With all my strength, I ran up to the door, and threw my body into the frame, only to get a big surprise. The lock, which had already been tampered with, dangled from the wooden door. The DEA had obviously beaten me to it. From there, I slowly pushed the door wide open, praying no one would jump out at me.

When I walked inside, I expected to see outlines drawn of where dead bodies use to lay. Instead, the room was mostly empty. With the exception of the wooden desk, and cardboard boxes scattered across the room, my eyes spotted nothing. I could hear Stacy calling my name from below, so I hurried over to the boxes, praying I'd find some money.

Again, nothing. Four matching boxes that read 'scales' caught my attention. I thought, *drugs*. Weighing fuckin' drugs! I hopped up and ran over to the walk-in closet, only to find safe nestled near the back wall. The door lay wide open with its hinges no longer in place.

"Damn," I said, kneeling to see if any money lay inside. Either the fuckin' DEA had it, or Samuel already had it stashed somewhere else.

I banged my hand on the floor, pissed that there was nothing for me to get when I heard Stacy. "Come on, Chanel," she yelled again.

I hurried from the room, leaving the door wide open. When my foot hit the bottom step, I felt relieved that we were gonna make it outta the house safely. I had my most important possessions, and enough clothes to last me for a few months. But then again, once the season changed, I'd be outta luck.

Stacy followed me toward the front door, still coaching me as she'd done for the last twenty minutes. "Chanel, sit the bags by the door. I'll handle those. Go through the garage and pull the car out."

"I will," I snapped. "Let's get these bags to the car first," I instructed, just as my right hand turned the knob on the door.

Instantly, a weird feeling crept through my skin. I thought I felt someone turning from the opposite side. At first, I considered my meds. Maybe they had me tripping or some shit. Then I tried again. I grabbed with force, yanked the door open, and almost fell out as Lou and I stood face to face. His height allowed our eyes to meet evenly. The fact that he wore a plain, black hoody and baggy jeans had me jumping outta my skin. My stomach felt queasy, and my body temperature rose ten degrees as he spoke.

"What the fuck you do to Samuel!" he screamed.

I swallowed hard, while he stood in the perfect Incredible Hulk looking stance, boiling with rage.

"Not a thing. W-h-y-y-y-y-y y-o-u h-e-e-e-e-e-r-r-r-r-e," I stuttered.

"I was trying to break in, but the question is…why the fuck are you here?"

"Ummm…ummm," I stuttered again, eyeballing the Home Depot bag in his hand.

"My man called me from jail talking about I was right. Something funky went down with your ass. I know it, and now he locked up. What did you do?" he scolded.

"I didn't do nothing!" I screamed, then breathed a sigh of relief. Although Lou was upset, Samuel obviously hadn't gotten a chance to tell him about the *real* me.

"If everything was intact with you, he wouldn't have called me to come change the locks over here and to call his lawyer. He woulda had you doing all of that." He glanced down at my bags, then his expression grew angrier. "You got Sam's money in those bags? Bring your ass here!" he hollered, and lunged at my neck.

I stumbled back, ready to pull my razor, but realized my purse was still in the car. Stacy screamed like a wild woman, but the next thing I knew, Lou had body slammed me into the frame of the door. I guess he thought his victory would come easy, but I had completely decided on saying, *fuck being a lady*.

I pushed him off me with all the strength I had. I felt like I was bench pressing 250, 'cause I was handling his big-ass. He charged me again, and I charged him back. It felt like he'd broken every bone in my body, but I never flinched. I could tell he was shocked, as he fought hard to wrestle me to the ground. We tossed and tussled for minutes, like two niggas in a street brawl.

Stacy's one scream when Lou first grabbed me, had now ceased. Her body remained stiff as she showed no reaction. Suddenly, I froze in my tracks when his arm stopped mid swing, and bawled his fist tightly. The muscles in his neck appeared to be popping from his veins. I knew I had to get down and ugly.

In the next instant, I noticed a strange car moving slowly through the cul-de-sac, gazing through a set of binoculars pointed dead at me. *Why the fuck are they still following me, especially if they let me go?* I wondered.

I glared at the car first, then Stacy's eyes followed too. Lou had no choice but to look. My only opportunity had come.

"Police!" I shouted.

I grabbed two of the bags and pushed Stacy along, jetting for the car. I'd already decided that if the police wanted to ask any more questions, they were gonna have to chase me down. I told Stacy's nervous–ass, who was now headed for the passenger side with me, to drive.

"What are you doing? Hurry, Stacy!" I shouted.

Luckily, she reacted quickly, and raced for the driver's side. I checked back over my shoulder to make sure Lou wasn't behind us. His dumb-ass was still standing in the doorway, watching the cops watch him.

Stacy did about ninety, racing outta the neighborhood with her hands clutching the steering wheel so tight, blisters were bound to appear. My heart sank as she pulled away from the only home I'd known since becoming a certified, full-fledged woman. I glanced over at my girl, hoping she could give me strength. Instead, I saw sweat bead up on her forehead, and her face appeared to be delusional. We both needed psychiatric help.

Suddenly, that same old feeling took over my body. Sharp pains played ping pong inside my stomach. I clutched at the lower part of my belly, but luckily Stacy didn't notice. She remained in her daze. I squirmed in my seat again just as I got hit with a gust of hot flashes. I rolled down my window, hoping the air would help. I couldn't keep from wondering if the pains were the same pains I'd gotten when staying at the hotel where Stacy worked.

"Oh shit," I mumbled to myself. "This shit may come back to haunt my ass."

For the first time since my operation, I was really convinced that the complications could possibly kill me. Two more minutes went by as my breathing intensified. Stacy finally took notice, and swerved over to the side of the road. I saw her putting the car in park, just as my eyes closed. Everything went black instantly. I do mean everything.

"Chanel!" she screamed.

I couldn't respond.

Chapter Eighteen

I awakened to the sounds of beeping machines and announcements being made over an intercom system. Slightly delirious about my whereabouts, I squinted and raised my head a bit, trying to make out the figure sitting next to me.

"Stacy," I whispered softly.

"Chanel, you okay?" she asked, with more concern than usual. Then scooted her chair closer to my hospital bed. "Gurllll, I was worried about your ass."

"How'd I end up here again?" I felt overly nauseous. "This is the hospital, right?"

She nodded. "That same problem from before. The doctor put some medication through your I.V to help you sleep. He said he'd come back once it wore off."

I closed my eyes for a quick second, and digested what Stacy had said. My body remained weak, yet my mind was becoming clearer. The I.V's were stuck in every available vein, and made me look as if I belonged in the intensive care unit. With a quick sigh of frustration, I threw the pillow over my face to keep the room from spinning.

"It'll be okay," Stacy assured me.

She rubbed my arm to verify that she had my back. I continued to lay still on the bed contemplating my life. My mind rewound back to when I was in my teens; that one night that probably changed my life. That fretful night still had me shook. I wondered if that moment had any bearing on my life-long decisions, and ultimately landed me in the hospital.

I remember that horrible night back in Detroit so

clearly. I'd just graduated from junior high, and thought I was the shit. My fan club had to have been longer than anyone else's at Paul Junior High, so I flirted with every beautiful girl who came in sight, trying to make my brother and his friends think I was a normal heterosexual boy.

The graduation party at my boy's house had been the talk of the town, so I had my chance to shine. I'd met a few girls at the party, but no one special, so I figured there was no need in upsetting my father by breaking my curfew. My brother had already left for another party with his crew, so I walked home all alone.

By the time I made it home, it was almost midnight. When I tip-toed past my parent's room, I wished I had stayed out longer, 'cause they hadn't even made it home from work yet. Once I made it to my room, my body collapsed on the bed, so I decided to lie on top of the covers, instead of taking my usual nightly shower. I remember that night being extremely hot, and my mother forbidding me to touch the air conditioner earlier in the day.

I fell asleep within minutes after opening up my Playboy magazine to check out Jennifer, who was my favorite playmate for the month. Seeing Jennifer's big juicy lips and neatly shaved pussy, always helped my young, growing dick mature back then. Or so I thought. Besides, the magazine was my personal therapy. I used it to help me become more attracted to women.

Hours later, I was face down sleeping peacefully, until my bedroom door squeaked a bit and opened slowly. I felt so exhausted my eyes felt like they weighed a ton. Besides, I knew it was my mother making sure I was home and in bed, which was normally her routine schedule..

As the footsteps grew closer, an eerie feeling told me to wake up. Something didn't seem right. My mother's footsteps were never that heavy. It didn't take long for the smell of my father's liquor-filled breath to fill the room.

I turned over quickly and called out to him. "What is it, Dad?"

He pulled a flask from down below his side and raised it to his drooling lips. As he took a sip, his shoulders hunched. He had a weird look on his face. A guilty look. An angry look.

"Did I do something wrong?" I asked.

He said nothing. He just dove on top of me. The bed shook, but my thin body lay hostage. I screamed and squirmed for a couple of seconds, hoping my mother had come home from work, or was nearby and would hear me. But after minutes of fighting off my father, no one came. I wasn't sure why he fought me like a grown man. "Get off me," I remember screaming. I pushed, shoved, squirmed, and kicked. Nothing worked.

At first I thought his drunken state had him delusional. I figured he didn't realize it was his son he was beating.

"Why?" I shouted. "Why are you doing this?"

Although he didn't answer, the minute he yanked at my pants, there was no need to question him anymore. I was only fourteen, but smart enough to know what he wanted. His weight seemed unbearable as pounded down on me. Somehow, he kept the palm of his large hand over my small-sized mouth, while he used his left hand to rip my pants completely down.

My dad had always been strong, but that night he used every muscle in his body to keep me pinned down. Before I knew it, he'd flipped me over onto my stomach and had my underwear down past my knees. I shouted as loud as I could when I realized his pants were down too, and felt his skin grazing my asshole.

"Daddy, no.......... please.....no, Daddy!" I yelled. But to no avail, my destiny was set.

When he entered me, it was a feeling I'd never forget.

I remember grunting in pain, and wondering what I'd done to deserve such harsh treatment. I continued to fight him, with my face buried into the pillow. However, my strength was no match.

My father lashed out saying, "Is this what you wanted? Is that what you looking for?" He'd even managed to press both my hands together above my head, with his over-powering left hand. He pounded and pounded inside my virgin asshole, grabbing me simultaneously by my neck. Each moment a slight breath of air passed through my nostrils, I'd scream a scream that I prayed would become louder, however, my sounds became more muffled instead. My face remained squashed down into the pillow, while my father continued to pump and groan on top of me.

Soon, I'd given up. I just flattened my body, with my soul stolen. My shouts turned to silence, while my struggle turned to tears. And finally, my silence turned to shame. I couldn't understand why he was doing this to me.

Although prior to the rape, comments were made about how I liked clothes way too much, feminine looking clothes at that. Or about how in my younger days, I preferred playing with dolls instead of the trucks my father piled into the living room. The suspicions about me soon increased. People had always said behind my back that I had homosexual tendencies, but my father would call me punks and bitches to my face.

I'm not sure what lesson he thought the rape would teach me, but I truly believe, that tragedy was the turning point in my life. From then on out, I was constantly mistaken for a bitch. Instead of running for a football, I wanted a set of pom poms. Instead of getting clear on my nails, I died for pink. Slowly, my life began to transform, month by month.

I went from simply perming my hair, to adding color and creating unique, girlish styles. My entire family could see a difference in me, especially my father. He called me every name in the book, from sissy to punk-ass to shim. I hated him for the names he'd call me. Plus, I double hated his guts for what he did to me, but never told a soul. 'Til this day it's a secret we'd both take to our grave. Often times, I wonder why my mother thinks he hates me so much.

"Miss Martinez, I'm Doctor Green," a pint-sized man said, interrupting my thoughts, and snapping his finger in front of my face.

I sniffled a bit and opened my eyes. The fact that the doctor had snapped me from my fretful flashback down memory lane, was probably a good thing. I wiped my tears away, and shot Stacy a fake grin.

"You okay?" she asked, with a frown.

"Yeah, just a little worried." I grinned again to reassure her.

"You should be," Dr. Green interjected.

The room went completely silent, until the machine beeped rapidly. It was probably the signal that I was going into cardiac arrest. I damn sho felt like it.

The doctor walked over to my machine that connected all my tubes, and punched a few buttons, clearing the machines. "Can we talk in private?" he asked. He turned briefly to give Stacy a funny look.

"Oh no,…she stays. She knows everything."

"Everything?" he questioned. His eyes opened widely.

"Everything," I confirmed.

"Well, let's get straight to the point. Your small intestines are inflated which means you have major issues, young lady. That's why you're experiencing the bleeding."

I breathed heavily. "So what does that mean in my world? Am I dying?"

"Oh no," he said, sitting down on the side of my bed. "First of all, I'll need to speak to your doctor who performed your operation."

"That might not be possible," I interrupted. "I had it done in Brazil."

"Ahhhh…I guess I don't have to ask why you went that far. You see what lean laws will do for you? Now we have even more problems without knowing your history from the surgery. Are you having problems with urinating too?"

I nodded with shame. "Just sometimes," I said sadly.

"I'm not sure how much they educated you before your procedure, but you should've known these problems would be a possibility. When they took your penis and inserted it inside of you to build your vaginal canal, it was created between your bladder, intestines, and your rectum. So they're all affected, which ultimately means your surgery could've been botched."

Something inside my head felt like it was now thumping against my brain. Stacy and I were both listening hard like med students taking lecture notes. Hell, this was scary enough just understanding, but even scarier, 'cause it was my life!

"What are my options for making this all better?"

"Can she change back into a man?" Stacy blurted out.

I shot her a look like she was crazy.

"Why the hell are you looking at me like that Chanel? Hell, I just want to know." Stacy responded.

"Oh nooooo. Absolutely not," Dr. Green snickered. "One option is to take blood thinners so no clotting will form and I'll subscribe another medication to help shrink your intestines. The first goal is to stop the bleeding."

"And if all else fails," I asked.

"I'll have to perform surgery."

"Surgery!" I shouted.

"For now, let's deal with one problem at a time. You'll be okay, but this will take some monitoring. And Chanel…"

"Yeah."

"No sex for the next two weeks, okay? I want to monitor everything closely."

I just nodded.

Doctor Green rose from the bed and made his way back to my machine. He punched a few buttons on the machine controlling my I.V. and scribbled a few notes on his clipboard.

"I want you to sleep a little more…you know rest a bit. I've started a slow drip of codeine to help with the stomach cramping. I'll release you tomorrow if all goes well."

I nodded again, while watching Dr. Green whisk his way through the door. Stacy decided to jump right in ready to take lead. She could tell I was speechless.

"Okay, here's the deal. You stay here and get better. Tomorrow I'll pull some money from my bank account and get us a hotel room until this Samuel shit blows over."

"Girl, I told you before, I'm not getting no hotel. Ain't no telling who Samuel got looking for me. Shit, I'm even scared to be in this hospital."

Stacy placed her hands on her hips. "Look, we can't live in my damn car! Now, like I said,… until all this stuff blows over, you're gonna stay in this hospital and take whatever medication the doctor prescribes so you can get better. Got it?"

"Got it." I managed to let a smile slip through the side of my cheek. "We girls for life?" Stacy asked me, getting all close up in my face.

"Of course."

"Real talk then…girl talk."

I knew she wanted the real get down kinda talk.

"Okay, Miss. I've got questions. Personal shit."

"Stacy, I hope you're sincere, 'cause I'm telling you things I've never told anyone before. I don't wanna end up on the Tyra Show. You really got my best interest, don't you?"

"I sure do. And I'm not here to judge. I only see black

and white."

"Good, 'cause I only see green. No, I'm just joking. But seriously, Stacy, I'm the color grey that's cool with everything and everybody. Girl, look no man can't judge me. We all have fucked up issues. Did you know that the average woman doesn't even like herself, let alone like others? So I don't expect to be accepted, just respected.

"Hallelujah." Stacy started having a good time with my lecture. She stood up and clapped her hands like she was at a church service, then reached over to give me a big hug.

Together we laughed our asses off.

"So, tell me…what's it like having sex, Chanel? I gotta know."

"It's g-o-o-o-o-d. That's what it's like. It is what it is." Then I laughed slightly. "The same way it feels for you, it feels for me."

"Okay, next. Where the hell is your Adam's Apple? I mean you look like you were born as a female, smooth skin and all."

"I had a tracheal shave. My Adam's Apple was carved down- so it's still there. It's just flat, so people don't know it's there."

"Damn, how'd you pay for all this shit?"

"Money girl. I had to shake this ass."

"Girl, I still can't believe you got a full fledge pussy. Just like mine."

"Yep, and a clit too."

"Damn, bitch. A clit too."

"Yep. They took the skin from my penis and made me a clit. Don't hate," I joked, beginning to feel the effects of the codeine.

"Can you feel sensations and the whole nine? I know when a nigga get to suckin' on my clit, it's over." Stacy high-fived me, and we laughed like crazy.

"Oh, I feel it."

"Damn, you must've spent some money."

"I sure did. $100,000 to be exact. Carlos, my old Suga Daddy paid for the bulk of my initial treatments. Hell, I know I've spent over $20,000 on my estrogen pills alone. That nigga Carlos, was undercover gay, so he wanted me to keep my dick. He never wanted me to go to Brazil," I announced, in a quieter tone. "Going all the way meant the end for us."

"Damn, estrogen, hormone pills…this shit is wild."

"Yeah, but that shit works. How you think I got a body like this?" I said, flipping the sheet off of me to expose my luscious shape. "The only thing they couldn't make look like a lady were my hands. That's why I'm so self conscious about 'em. Never want them to be seen or touched."

"Umph…umph…umph…" Stacy uttered. "I can't get past the hormone pills shit and all they can do."

"Yeah. Check it. I need them damn pills, 'cause one week I wanted pussy for breakfast and dick for dinner." I stopped to think about how crazy that bi-sexual shit sounded. "I think I'm stable now though, 'cause I loves me some Samuel," I confessed, in a lower voice. "I wish he would just accept who I've become."

"Was it worth it?" Stacy asked, pulling my sheet back up to my neck.

"Was what worth it?"

"You know…the operation. Do you ever regret it?" she asked in a more serious tone.

"No, I don't regret my decision. Shit, at least I made one. Most people who've walked in my shoes have committed suicide. I embraced a new life. Unfortunately, I chose the wrong person to live the rest of it with; a hot boy. Any how, I'm happy with who I am, and could care less about how others perceive me. We all have one life to live, and I chose two. It's a wonderful life to know how a man thinks and feels, yet honored to understand the mechanics of a woman."

"So, speaking of dicks, I have to ask. How big was yours?"

Even though I really didn't want to answer the question, I knew Stacy wouldn't let up. "Let's just say this…I was definitely packing. At least nine inches."

Stacy shook her head. "Damn, a big dick gone."

"Just because a man may have nine to twelve inches, after three inches of hitting the G spot, the rest is a waste anyway! Don't get me wrong, Miss Stacy, yes I do need my men packing heavy artillery. But at the end of the day, men and women have more in common than what they really know. It's all mental and fucked emotions. It is what it is."

"Okay, so the biggie. Why did Samuel think you were pregnant? I know technology ain't like that."

"Oh, girl, that baby was birthed from mere panic. I told Samuel that because he questioned my cycle. But just know that having a baby doesn't make you a woman. It makes you a mother."

Stacy gave me a ton of Amens and shouts, like I was a serious pastor. And after that long sermon, I felt myself struggling to keep my eyes open. The doctor said the meds would be a slow drip, but hell, I felt like I'd taken 1,000 milligrams of Morpheme.

"Stacy," I called out.

"Yeah, Chanel. What is it?" She grabbed my hand tightly.

"I think my hormones are acting up again."

"Why you say that?"

"It's just a confusing situation. My body, mind, and everything is still adjusting." I looked her dead in the eye. "'Cause I think I'm falling in love with you."

Stacy dropped my hand and hit me with a strong gasp. "Cut that shit out, Chanel."

185

"I'm serious," I mumbled. With a slight smile, I closed my eyes and dozed off to sleep.

Chapter Nineteen

Three days later, I found myself pacing the floor in my temporary home. The Hampton Inn, in downtown ATL, was the safest and cheapest place for me to lay my head. When I checked in, the guy at the counter tried to hit us with $189.00 per night.

"Like hell," I told him, while I flirted a little bit, to get the best discount possible. His eyeballs were buried in my chest, so I winked at Stacy, letting her know it would be okay.

When Stacy picked me up from the hospital and showed me where she'd been staying, I remember telling her to pull off. There was no way I was going back to staying in dumps again. While the Hampton Inn wasn't the Westin, it was doable. At least it was clean, and only ended up costing us only $100.00 a night. I just felt bad that Stacy had an apartment she was scared to even go back to. It seemed so unbelievable that Samuel had us afraid to even sleep through the night. I knew I had to find out his status, 'cause our money was running low. Real low. If I didn't come up with a plan by sundown, we'd have to go relocate to a damn Motel 6, Super 8, or even a truck stop. I cringed at the thought.

I thought about the fact that I'd gotten myself right back into the same situation once again. *Broke, with nowhere to go*. I looked over at Stacy, who had plopped down into the flowery outdated lounger, and thought, she'd always been broke. But happily broke. Stacy had always made just enough to barely get by. But I'd taken her to another level, where she didn't wanna go to work, or even pass by her job. Being on the run was some bullshit.

"I gotta foot the bills," I said to myself. "I'm the one who got us in this shit." I paced the floor even more, thinking about my options for coming up with some cash.   Stacy yelled out, "Chanel, please stop it," you're driving me crazy!"

I didn't respond. I just stopped in the middle of my next stride, and pressed the button on the small 25 inch television. I figured maybe a little noise in the room would occupy Stacy for a moment, which would keep her from staring me down.

"I'm sorry for yelling at you Chanel. I know you got problems, but I'm trying to sit here and pray cause we need it."

For some reason, Pastor Joe Scott popped into my head. I still needed to get him out of the way, just in case Samuel and I reconciled. Then it dawned on me. That plan would have to be put on hold. I had no money, so what could I possibly conjure up without cash. Nobody would help me for free. I banged myself against my head, as my thoughts became all jumbled. I had too much on my plate; too much to handle. Too many problems.

Samuel, I thought. My issues with him were way more important than thinking about the pastor. I rushed over to the side of the bed and grabbed my cell phone off the charger. I pulled out the card the DEA agent, Jerri had given me, and dialed his number. I had to find out what happened with Samuel. At least if he was still locked up, I'd feel a little better about moving around town.

As the phone rang, my heart rate sped. I felt unbelievably nervous for even calling to find out what happened to him. When Jerri answered, I could barely speak.

"Hello, hello, hello," Jerri kept repeating into the phone.

"Uhh…it's Chanel Martinez," I finally said.

"Oh, so you finally came to your senses, huh? Where are you?"

His question caught me off guard. Why did he need to know my whereabouts? Was he on Sam's payroll?
"Ahh…I'm around. I didn't get to make the arraignment. And my husband won't answer his cell phone. So, I figured he did-n't get out, but wanted to check for sure."

"Oh, I see," he muttered, like he didn't believe me. "Well, he's out alright. Been out for two days now."

A lump formed in my throat. "Two days?" I needed confirmation, just to be sure I heard him correctly.

"So, I take it you haven't seen him? His bond was $500,000. Some big shot lawyer strolled into court, and got the judge to agree to give him bail."

My eyes seemed to roll toward the back of my head. *Shit, shit, shit,* I thought.

"So, you wanna come in and talk?"

"Not really sure. I gotta go," I said in a hurry, and just clicked the end button on my phone.

My body temperature had risen. The feeling of a bad virus caught me right in the middle of my belly. I leaned slightly onto the bed, resting my weight on my elbows. Stacy glared into thin air. I didn't know if she was praying or just thinking. At times, she was the strong one, then at other times, she became my little sister, who I'd have to take care of.

"Stacy," I shouted.

"Yeah," she answered, glassy eyed and all.

"Samuel is out," I said slowly.

Her bottom lip dropped low, and she reacted just like she'd seen something out of a horror movie. "How you know?"

"Trust me. It's true. I just hung up from the agent I told you about from down at the station."

"So, I guess you'll be getting a call from Samuel."

Just then, I thought about checking my missed calls. Maybe he'd called while we were sleeping. I pressed the button and scrolled the list, praying I'd see a missed call from him, or even a number that wasn't known. *Wishful thinking. Nothing. No one.*

Instinct told me to hop up. I leaped from the bed, patting the sweat from my face, and rushed to the bathroom to tidy up a bit. My hair didn't look half as fresh as I normally kept it, but it had to do for now. There was no money for a hair-do at the moment. Before I knew it, I'd thrown on what was left of my foundation. My eye concealer was already completely gone, and the mascara was dwindling too. I knew I had to make money, and thought of the best place to start.

"Stacy, lets go," I ordered in an anxious tone. I developed a confident, quick strut as I grabbed my purse, and thought about how I had to make my own way. I was tired of relying on other people to give me the life I wanted.

"Where we going?" Stacy asked.

"Look, I gotta go make us some money, so we can afford this place a few more nights."

"How the hell are you gonna make money?"

I looked deep into her eyes. "I been a survivor all my life. This ain't no different, other than Samuel might wanna kill my ass." I thought about how he never even flinched when I told him I'd killed Essence by mistake, which wasn't surprising. Killing folks was a part of his everyday lifestyle. Whatever it took for him to stay on top, was exactly what he'd do, without any remorse.

"Let's go," I said, once again to Stacy. I held the hotel door open as she walked slowly past me.

"Chanel, can you tell me where we're going?"

"You'll see." Give me your damn keys. You're not capable of driving right now," I ended, with a slam of the door.

***

When we pulled up to Magic City, Stacy opened her eyes in shock. She sat up straight in her seat. "Is this how you gonna make some money?" she asked in a tone, letting me know she disapproved.

"Gotta do what I gotta do." I wanted to say my favorite, *it is what it is*, but that shit had gotten me into too much trouble over the last year.

"I'll wait here," Stacy said, leaning over in the seat, and closing her eyes again.

"Suit yourself."

I hopped out, checked my surroundings, and jetted inside. My feet moved swiftly through the double doors. I looked behind me one last time, making sure DEA, Samuel, Lou, or whoever else wasn't trailing me. Once inside, the funky smell of sweat and unclean pussy hit me right in the face. Instantly, I scanned the room looking for Willy. I had to convince him to let me do a few sets tonight.

As I moved through the club, a few of my regulars showed me love by immediately calling out my name.

"Sunshine, baby. Get up there on that stage and show 'em how to get this money."

Another tall guy with a goatee, just held a twenty dollar bill in the air, making sure our eyes connected.

I could smell the money and couldn't wait to get back on the stage. I continued to look around until I saw Big Willy standing near the stage, wearing an Emmitt Smith football jersey that was three sizes too small. He didn't notice me walking up on him, 'cause he was busy checking out some girl on stage that I'd never seen before.

"Willy," I called to him.

He turned at the sound of my voice unexcitedly. He was all tight-faced like I'd done something to him. "What'cha need?"

"Damn, is it like that?" I placed my hands on my hips.

He shrugged his shoulders and looked back toward the stage.

The upbeat of the music seemed to get louder, so I raised my voice a bit.

"Willy, I need my job back."

"Huh. That's funny. You shoulda thought about that before sending your boyfriend down here to make threats."

"What? I didn't know nothing about that."

"You sent him to get your check, didn't you?"

"Yeah, but that was it. I didn't tell him to make no threats."

"Well, he did," Willy announced, in a matter of fact tone. "Look, I got some things I gotta take care of." He turned in the direction of his office, leaving me standing there looking stupid.

My feet shuffled rapidly to catch up with him. I grabbed Willy by the arm, with just enough strength to slow him down a bit. "Look, Willy, whatever Samuel said to you, I apologize. He's just so possessive. But I really need my job back."

"Is that so?"

"Yes." My eyes pleaded with him.

"You left me when I needed you most. Some of my customers even thought you went to work at another club. Some of them ain't been back." He stopped to take a deep breath, while I watched his stomach inflate and deflate, as he breathed heavily. "Look, don't take this shit personal. I just can't have you back."

"Because of my jealous boyfriend? Well, actually he's my husband now," I said, getting on the defensive.

"Who gives a fuck who he is to you, and it's not just that. I'ma be honest. I want no parts of this investigation bullshit."

"What the hell are you talking about?"

"That Essence bullshit. Detectives been coming here questioning me and some of the girls about her being missing. They think she's dead!"

My entire face went flush. I swallowed hard, keeping my poker face tight. "I'm not sure where Essence is…"

Big Willy cut me off. His expression changed. He now looked at me like some criminal. "Tiger told the cops you was with them the night before she disappeared, and was still with Essence when she left her place. Nobody has seen her since."

My stance changed. I got on the defensive tip, and folded my arms across my chest. Worry filled my insides. "So?"

"So? That's all you gotta say?" He laughed slightly. "You better come better than that with the police. I ain't gonna front. I gave 'em the only info I had on you, and that was a copy of your drivers license."

At that point, my mind scrambled overtime. I couldn't even remember what license I'd given Willy when I got hired.

"So, you don't know where Essence could be?" Willy badgered.

"No, I don't."

"Were you with her like Tiger said you were?"

I kept my answers short and sweet. "No. Look, are you gonna let me work or not?"

"Not," he said bluntly.

"Sucka-ass nigga," I mumbled under my breath.

I hated a man who couldn't be a man. At least I knew my place, and just became a full-fledged woman. I laughed to myself picturing, Big Willy's fat-ass on the table getting a sex change.

Before I turned to walk away, I shouted, "You'll wish you had me on that stage when I start working for your competition!"

I walked out of Magic City with my head held high, taking in all the compliments from the guys as I stepped. I promised myself I wouldn't think about the fact that the police could be on to me. I promised myself that I wouldn't break down and cry.

When the outside air hit me in the face, I decided I would make Stacy think everything would be okay. A bitch needed money, and had to jump back into survival mode. Besides, she'd only asked me about Essence once since her disappearance. I brushed if off, but certainly couldn't tell Stacy the police was now asking questions about Essence's disappearance, nor the fact that they wanted to talk to me.

Quickly, I put my shades on, trying to camouflage my face just in case somebody was watching. When I hopped in the car, Stacy was on the phone talking to some chick from Marietta, which was cool, 'cause I didn't wanna look her in the face anyway. Especially when I knew there was some important information that I was deliberately keeping from her. I zoomed out the parking lot like a mad-woman trying to map out my next move. While Stacy talked to her girl, I contemplated something that was my craziest idea yet. I whipped out my cell and dialed.

With complete surprise, he answered on the first ring.

"Samuel?" I asked, with a blank expression. I swerved the car into the CVS parking lot on Fairfield Road, and hopped out like the car was on fire. This was one conversation Stacy didn't need to hear.

"Samuel, baby, I'm glad you got out."

"Don't fuckin' call me baby. I'm not your baby. I want you to know that I will not be the laughing stock of Atlanta! You feel me?"

His tone was so different. Assertive, yet chilling. I'd seen him at his worst, but this was sort of mental. Hurt filled

195

his voice.

"Sam, let me explain." I circled the car for the second time, while Stacy watched from inside.

"No need to explain. You betrayed me. You had me fucking a man! But guess what? None of my boys will ever know about this!" he shouted into the phone.

I inched my cell away from my ear just a bit, 'cause Samuel was going off. His angry demeanor had changed into a wild outburst.

"Listen....and listen good," he finally stopped to say. His heavy breathing slowed just a bit. "The DEA agents said you committed to testifying against me."

"I didn't," I interrupted.

"I may have to go to trial, but trust and believe you won't be there."

"I'm your wife, Samuel," I cried out. I couldn't believe he'd made an official threat.

"No, Terell. You're not. You're my enemy. You set out to hurt me. Now, I gotta hurt you!"

"No......Samuel...noooooooo! Pleaseeeeeee, don't."

Click was all I heard. He'd obviously ignored my pleas.

I stampeded my way back around the car, opened the door, and slammed it with a vengeance. Stacy had a blank look on her face, as I explained that we were officially on the run. I told her that Samuel wasn't after her, and that I thought she should stay away from me.

Her response, "Chanel, you my girl. I'm with you all the way."

I removed my shades and covered my face leaving only my eyes exposed. "I gotta do something," I said, rocking back and forth in the seat.

Suddenly, it came to me. I grabbed my cell and dialed Pastor Joe Scott's number. When he answered, my skin felt an immediate twinge. It was a creepiness I couldn't explain. Within seconds, I'd fed him a days worth of bullshit, and told him where we'd meet the following day.

I hung up, shaking my head, while my hands shook nervously. I silently prayed that my new hair-brained scheme would work.

Chapter Twenty

I seldom came out of the hotel room unless I had to, but my latest idea was crucial. One, we needed to pay for another night before check-out time, so I had the trunk of Stacy's Altima open at 9 a.m. in the center of the Hampton Inn parking lot, selling my best gear. My first sale of fifty bucks was made by 9:15 a.m., but sadly, I had to sell my favorite pair of Dolce & Gabbana thigh-high boots.

Money had started to become tighter and tighter. My meds were getting low; but essential, so that I wouldn't end back up in the hospital or on somebody's operating table. I needed to re-up as soon as I earned enough money for a few more nights of hotel stays. Food was secondary though. Hell, I always ate light anyway, just trying to keep my shape in tact. But hell, I was beginning to worry about Stacy. Too many days of McDonald's dollar menu items wasn't wearing well on her.

I flinched as a tall, fair-skinned man walked up on me unexpectedly. "Whatchu selling?" he asked, reminding me of Samuel in the face.

"What you see is what you get." I waved my hand in the direction of the clothes and footwear like Vanna White. The items were laid out neatly in the trunk. A few pieces were even folded over top of my Louie V. duffel bags. I was really trying to do some creative merchandising.

"How much for this shirt?" he asked.

"Gimme twenty," I quickly responded.

He shook his head. Not interested obviously.

I didn't waste anymore time on him. When I spotted a hotel employee darting from inside over to her car, I waved her over to the trunk. She looked at me strangely, trying to figure out what I wanted. My presence seemed to intimidate her a little, so I eased up on my assertive sales technique.

"Girl, I just broke up with my boyfriend, so I'm selling all this shit he bought me," I snickered, trying to sound believable.

The petite sized woman waltzed over, while my tall friend still fumbled around with one of my shirts. My mind tried to quickly itemize what I had to fit the petite sized broad.

While she looked through the limited amount of inventory, my tall customer asked me something I didn't expect to hear. "How much for the Louie bags?"

"Oh…those aren't for …" I stopped mid-sentence. "$700," I called out.

"$200," he shot back.

"No way. Give me $300.00," I pressed.

"Here…they're yours." I threw my perfectly placed shirts off the top in a dash, and handed the bags to him, hoping he would take them.

Before I knew it, he'd taken the bags, given me the cash, and made my day. The petite woman even bought a chain that I had on display, hanging across the spare tire. It hurt me to my heart to see my duffel bags go.

As the gentleman walked away, I should've been happy. I'd accomplished my goal, and had enough cash to keep us going for a few more days, but for some reason I was still depressed. When he turned to ask me one last question, I figured I was a complete idiot for saying no.

"How much for the ring?" he asked.

I looked down at my diamond ring, thinking Samuel. Oh hell no, there's still a chance. I love that man. How could I sell the only thing I had left of him?

"It's not for sale," I finally uttered.

***

It only took about twenty minutes to close up shop, count my profit, and pay our bill in the hotel lobby. After making a few phone calls, I even had an order of pancakes and eggs sent up to Stacy, before jetting out the parking lot on two wheels. I didn't think twice about eating. I had money on my mind, and my mind on my money.

My meeting had been set for eleven o'clock sharp, and for a Wednesday, traffic seemed pretty thick. The Hilton Garden Inn, our trusty meeting spot, hadn't changed. I was just about five minutes away, when I looked down at my ringing cell phone. The screen read 'private'.

I held the wheel tightly with my left hand, and answered with my right, wondering if it was Samuel calling with another threat. I checked my rear-view mirror as I said hello. For some strange reason, I just felt all gooey inside, like somebody was following me.

"Hello," I said hesitantly.

No response came from the other end.

I repeated myself slower and drove even faster. "Hello, hello...hello."

Still nothing, until I heard the sound of someone hanging up.

Nervously, I fumbled with the phone, which fell to the floor beneath my foot. I didn't bother trying to grab it, 'cause now I was on pins and needles, wondering who'd called me playing on the damn phone.

By the time I'd pulled into the parking lot, I was a nervous wreck. I circled the lot at least three times, before getting out and heading to the room. Joe had texted me the room number, so I knew exactly where to go. When I passed the ice machine, I nearly jumped at the loud sound of ice being made in the machine. I stopped and peeped over the railing just to make sure nobody was behind me.

I knocked three times before Joe opened the door, wearing an out-dated blue polyester shirt.

His ass is still country as hell, I thought as I walked in. I made sure to create a face that had an extra worried look. I had my plan altogether, just needed him to buy it. Instead of focusing on my facial expression, Joe's eyes zoomed in on my form-fitting t-shirt that made my breasts scream for attention. It seemed like he remained in a daze, unable to re-focus.

I sat on the bed, and threw my hands in the air. "Look, I know what you wanna do, but I think we need to talk."

He came closer, still drooling over my body. "Talk, sweetness."

I sat up tall with a straight face and acted as though I was so distraught. "Lou and Samuel told the police that you were the last one to be with Essence."

His face held an immediate concern. "You gotta be kidding me!"

"No…and that's not it. I think the detectives are looking for you for questioning. Probably gonna go by your church."

He glared into my eyes with worry, wondering why they would do something like that to him. "Why me?" he asked.

"That's just Samuel. By any means necessary. He just got out on bond for all kinds of murder, and drug trafficking charges. Check the records if you don't believe me."

Joe's face turned a light shade of purple. "Don't they know I could turn everybody in. Even you," he said, in a panic.

My back arched, as I tried to feel him out. "Me?"

"I was the one on Essence's phone when you and

Essence were arguing," he revealed. "She hung up the line eventually, but I ran over to the place later after not hearing back from her. She was supposed to convince the three of us to have a threesome," he announced, with shame.

I looked at him, as if to say, tell it all.

"There was no answer, so I left. That evening, I went back and sat out front, and watched Lou go into Essence's house. I was shocked to see him there. I just assumed they had a thing going on, but the crazy thing is, I never saw him leave." He shrugged his shoulder while rubbing his forehead. "I thought maybe he left out a back door or something even though I don't know if there's a backdoor. But I do know that Essence wasn't there when I went back to knock after that. Nobody's seen her since," he said, in a creepy voice.

I kept a straight face and pretended to be shocked at what I was hearing. "Look, Samuel killed Essence. He's crazy like that. He was jealous and thought Essence was trying to steal me from him."

Joe made his way to the bed, taking a seat beside me. I could tell his mind boggled with questions. "You know, Samuel was never really into real estate. It was his front. Just know that he's capable of anything."

I swung my arm around Joe's upper backside, and caressed his back affectionately. I needed to go in for the kill. I figured he was eighty percent on my side, but I needed to be sure. If the police ever came at me with murder charges, Joe saying he saw Lou leaving Essence's place would set me straight.

By this time I knew Joe wanted sex. But the doctor had already made it clear, no sex. So I had to use my other tools. Joe needed to trust me fully. Plus, I needed to get hit off with about eight hundred.

Handling business was what I'd become accustomed to. So within seconds, I'd hit the floor, and got on my knees.

Joe saw me coming, so he opened his legs widely, welcoming me, and leaned back just a bit. Once, I scooted down in between his thighs, and pecked at his chest, Joe's stiff dick poked me in the face. I tugged at his unattractive pants, that were made out of some weird material, that I couldn't even identify. However, Joe decided to lift his body and yanked his pants down on his own.

I grabbed his stiffness with force, and commenced to sucking like a professional. Joe seemed to melt immediately. His head bobbed backwards, unable to watch me handle my biz. His ooohs and aaahs at least showed me he was still coherent.

I tried to stop thinking about Samuel, but couldn't. He was the man who should've benefited from my fabulous lip service. I just closed my eyes, and worked his dick, like the professional I was.

Joe started pulling my head toward him with force, ready to explode as I just kept sucking on his dick for what seemed like an eternity. He started lifting from the edge of the bed, going into convulsions, while I sucked faster, like I needed to win the fastest dick-sucking record. Before I knew it, Joe had nutted all over the bedspread. I jumped back, thinking, *I'd seen those specials on T.V., the maids probably wouldn't even wash the comforter*.

Joe stood up with a hungry expression, never even attempting to wipe his nasty ass. His eyes revealed that he wanted more, while his hardening rod confirmed it. I had to think quickly. There was no way my body could take dick inside of me. The doctor said no, and I needed to say no.

It wasn't long ago when I seemed to be clever than most. Now it seemed as though, I'd lost my touch.

"Wait," I called out. I extended my hand into thin air. I started sniffling, and shedding real tears.

"Ahhh...nooooo...here we go again," he said. "You

thinking about your brother?"

"No," I cried. If awards were being given out for best actress, I would've gotten two. "Nobody understands," I sobbed even more. I covered my face and twirled around the room, acting like I couldn't take anymore.

"Okay, I'll tell you what. Let's finish up here, then we can sit and talk about it," he suggested, in a consoling voice.

"I can't finish up!" I snapped. "I'm having flash-backs."

I peeped from behind my hands that remained over my face. I had his attention, but needed to finish the job. "I was raped as a child. And whenever I have flashbacks, I can't have sex. I just go crazy. I think I need help. A psychiatrist, or something."

Joe started to change his demeanor. His expression softened drastically. Something I'd never seen in him before. "You know I've got a confession too," he uttered.

My eyes opened widely, just as my hands dropped from my face.

Joe sat down on the bed, and reached for his pants as he spoke. "I was raped as a child too. Twelve to be exact."

The room became silent. Although I wanted to know the details, I figured from sadness the in his eyes, he needed a moment.

"You know, I figured that since I'd discovered God's word, I would forget. I guess I forgave, but will never forget." He looked up at me, to see how I was taking all of this.

I was speechless. I decided to shake the embarrassment off by fixing myself up.

"Chanel, I'll tell you. I wasn't always sinning, forni-cating, and acting like this. It comes in spurts. At times, I think I'm over this sexual addiction. But lately, I just can't kick this bad sex habit. I know in my heart, it's because of that tragic event."

"So, who raped you?"

"A friend of the family. He used to keep me and my sister from time to time."

"You'll be okay," I said softly.

"I think I got a problem, Chanel. I crave sex. Crave it all the time," he confessed. I like dressing up, doing different stuff. Wild, exotic, sexual things. And I know it's wrong."

I listened on.

"I just gotta stop. Get some help. That's why I stopped going over to Magic City."

"Do you fuck men too?" I said, in the most comforting voice I could muster.

He looked at me and smiled. "I fucked you, right?"

It was at that moment, when I realized he must've known my secret all along. "How did you find out?"

"Essence showed me your pills."

I let out a heavy sigh. "So, why did you go along with everything? Why didn't you tell Samuel?"

"Because I don't give a shit. Man...woman, as long as I can get my dick sucked, who cares."

I looked at him like he'd lost his mind. "Look, I guess rape affects us all differently. I do need a good woman to settle down with, and make her my wife."

I didn't comment on that wife situation, 'cause his look said that he was considering me. After he pulled his pants up, we talked for nearly an hour. I gave him the truthful version about how my father had raped me, and I listened to his entire story.

We ended our conversation on a good note, with Joe saying he was gonna turn his life around, and turn a negative into a positive. We also discussed how to deal with Lou and Samuel. My plan worked well, until Joe went into his pockets to give me some money.

"I don't wanna pay for what just happened with us," he

said. "I've got a whole new outlook on life now."

"Yeah that's all good, Joe. But you need to have that attitude after I get my damn loot.

Reluctantly, he handed me $400 in a crumbled up wad. It wasn't what I expected, but shit I couldn't complain.

"Where are you staying?" he asked.

"With Stacy. As a matter of fact, take down her number, just in case I disappear like Essence."

Joe frowned, I guess thinking about Samuel and Lou. "We'll be in touch," he said, nodding toward me.

"If anything happens to me. Be sure to tell the police."

"You stay outta their way. I'm certainly gonna lay low. And pray, I might add."

I smiled for the first time in days, and walked out the door. When the door shut, I jumped up high and balled my fist, congratulating myself on a job well done.

Chapter Twenty One

The next morning, I got up early once again, and commenced to doing the stupidest thing I could've done. I made my way over to Monica's salon, to get my weave washed and curled. Truth be told, a totally new weave was needed, but my money situation required a major boost. *$500.00 hair from Malaysia...umph, that used to be what I could afford.*

The mid-day sunlight was already creeping in on me, so a call to Stacy was needed. I'd borrowed her car, and told her we'd meet up at the hotel by noon. I'd already spent most of the morning scouting out a few strip joints on the outskirts of ATL, but finally decided to go back to Jaycees, since they were willing to give me a chance.

I wanted to let Stacy know that I'd gotten the job, so when she saw my hair, she wouldn't freak out, and complain about me spending money on unnecessary shit. *Hell, you gotta spend money to make money, and I damn sho gotta look good to pull in the dollars at the club*, I thought. Besides, the club was my secondary plan. Plan A would really get me paid. I just needed the right clientele.

While Monica took the last few rollers from the back of my hair, I whipped out my phone and called Stacy. The phone rang several times, until the sound of her voicemail came on.

"Stacy, call me back," I said, in an irritated voice. I wondered where she could've been. Most mornings, I'd get up trying to figure out how to get money, while she'd lounge around in a state of depression. For the moment, I assumed she was either at the hotel, or on her way back from her apartment. She needed to let the rental office know the already late rent would be paid within a few days. Stacy told me she would catch a cab if she decided to go, so I needed her little ass to call me. I needed to know that she was okay.

I thought about my next call to Cheryl. I wanted to make sure my credit cards were sent overnight, like she proclaimed. Although Cheryl had always been about her business, she was too inaccessible for me. I'd sent her the money through Western Union the day before, and all she said to me was the cards would be delivered by FedEx before noon. Before I could ask her how many, the tracking number, or anything else, she'd hung up on my ass.

When I used to deal with her back in Detroit, she treated me the same way. However, the only difference was that she knew I was in the same town, and would kick her ass if she stiffed me. Now, being in ATL, I just had the funny feeling she wasn't gonna make good on our deal.

I dialed the bitches number, while the steam from the hot-ass curlers scorched my scalp. *Beauty was known to be painful, and sooooooo necessary, so I didn't say shit. I just flinched a little.*

"Cheryl," I said, through the phone, as soon as she answered. "Did you send my shit?"

She cursed my ass out in what seemed like two different languages. "Bitch, when I say it's on the way, it's on the way," she barked.

I let her slide with the bitch remark 'cause truth be told, I needed her ass...bad. "You did send the package to the hotel, right?" I asked, with concern.

" Remember...I don't do too much talking over the phone."

"Look, I gotta get the clothes 'cause..."

The sound of her hanging up on me caught me off

guard.

I wanted to start shouting and cursing like a sailor, but when Monica asked me what clothes I was talking about on the phone, I figured it was a good selling opportunity. I didn't even waste time lying. I told her that I had a few credit cards on the way, and was gonna purchase some high-dollar shit to sell for half off. She seemed excited and confirmed that she was down, and had seen a short leather jacket in Neiman's just the other day that she wanted.

"Bet, I can get it," I said with confidence.

"But your ass can forget that fifty percent off shit Chanel. You stealing the stuff anyway, so I need at least seventy percent off."

My face held a deep frown. "Monica, who the fuck do you think I am? A crackhead or some shit? I'm a businesswoman in case you didn't know."

"Umph." She shrugged her shoulders. "Well, you must not want my business."

Monica and I continued to talk, while she ran down a long list of chicks she thought would be interested in some hot clothes, at a *can't refuse price*. She revealed that she wanted kickbacks too. I thought, *a kick in the ass was all she'd get*. But I listened in a reserved manner, so that I could snatch her connections with her clients and friends. By the time we finished talking, she'd called three girls for me, and I got a good idea of the type of shit I had to get for them.

When I got up from the chair, the mirror caught me with a smile. *I'm back*, I thought to myself. My tresses flowed to the middle of my back, and my new connections were gonna get me some money. All I needed now was some make-up, and a few new outfits to look good for my first set.

"I'll be in touch as soon as I get the shit," I told Monica. I passed her two twenties in the palm of her hand and walked toward the door.

"What the hell is this?" she shouted.

"Oh…I'll take care of you later when we meet up with the clothes."

"Chanel, you're tripping now!" she yelled.

I opened the door and walked out the salon without even looking back. I did however, check my surroundings making sure I hadn't been followed.

My next stop; back to the hotel to see if my package had arrived. As I headed down the highway in Stacy's car, my mind raced thinking about how much money I could make. I needed more clientele, and more money to keep things flowing. Most importantly, I had to make my own way.

When I pulled up into the hotel parking lot, I smiled seeing the FedEx driver pass me. I flagged him down, admiring how handsome he looked.

"Hey, did you just deliver something to Dawn Woods?" I asked, giving him the fake name in which the package should've been addressed to. I hopped out of the car, with my door still wide open.

"That depends on who's asking?" He smiled, giving me his best seductive look, and moved closer to the opening in his truck.

"I'm Dawn," I grinned. "Seriously, did you just deliver something for me?"

"I'm serious too, sexy. Can I get your phone number, Miss Dawn?"

His biceps bulging beneath his corny purple and black uniform, excited me a tad. But just the thought of dating somebody who worked for FedEx had me vexed. I needed to be wined and dined.

"By the way, I'm Ray," he said, as I watched his thick lips move in slow motion. He extended his hand for a shake, while reaching over his shoulder to grab his business card.

He's sexy as hell! I grabbed the card from his hand. I

read it, and arched my neck a little. I was shocked. *Real Estate Agent. Oh, hell no. Not again*, I thought.

"Why you looking like that?" he asked. "I know how to take good care of a woman." He grinned again.

"Oh really? Well, maybe you can show me sometime." It felt good to flirt again.

I slipped Ray's card into my back pocket just as Lou's green Toyota Camry shot by me. Stacy sat in the passenger seat holding her hands sheepishly in the air, as if she wasn't sure whether to wave or bang on the window. Everything seemed to move in slow motion. When Lou's face caught my eye, it reminded me of a scene from a horror movie. While I stared at him, he shot me back with an even nastier stare, confirming that he wasn't there for a friendly visit.

Worry filled my face, as I looked in Stacy's direction. Lou's car pulled to the side of the hotel away from the other cars. "I'll call you Ray," I ended, dashing away quickly.

Ray could tell my mind was now occupied with something else by the way I fixed my eyes on the screeching Camry, and moved closer to Stacy's car. He rushed behind the wheel leaving me with a smile. "Yeah, Dawn I'll talk to you soon!" he yelled and pulled off.

I hopped back behind the wheel nervously, ready to confront Lou. Within seconds, I drove over toward the passenger side of his car, and hopped out, yelling like a mad woman. Luckily, we were on a secluded side of the hotel, and only two other cars were parked near us. Besides, not many people were coming and going.

Instantly I got buck, hunching my shoulders back, like a throw down was eminent. Stacy's eyes protruded as she pointed through the window in my direction. I had to help my girl, but it seemed like she wanted to help me instead. I ignored her at first until fear overshadowed her face. She seemed to be reaching for the handle in a panic when an arm reached around my neck, and strangled me from behind.

With my head yanked backward, far enough toward my assailant, I finally caught a glimpse of his face and twisted expression. It was a scowl that I'd never seen before. I screamed, "Get off of me!" hoping someone would hear me.

Samuel's feet shuffled behind me like he was trying to lift me from the ground slightly. The closeness of his body gave me an eerie feeling; just like the smell of his breath close to my face. Strangely, I wanted him close, but the way he pulled with force, he needed to loosen his grip a bit. In a dash, he inched me along toward a beige Ford Taurus, gripping my wrist with all his might.

"Shut the fuck up," he said, shoving me inside the passenger side of the car.

I hit my head on the inside roof, trying to resist. When I saw the door being slammed in my face, I took one last shot at a loud scream, just in case someone noticed what was going down. Unfortunately, there was still nobody nearby, other than Stacy and Lou to hear my shouts.

Damn, why didn't Ray stick around? "Where are you taking me?" I shouted from inside.

I reached for the door ready for my escape, when Samuel lifted his shirt outside my door, exposing his nine millimeter. That was code for, *don't move!*

He rushed to the other side, while I stayed put, contemplating my next move. Jumping out of the car became my first option. I figured as soon as he hit a busy street, a jump-out move, would set me free.

Once the car started, I watched Stacy as she finally escaped from Lou's car, and raced across the parking lot headed toward the hotel lobby. Stacy ran so fast, she could've won a gold medal at the Olympics. Lou looked pissed, but chasing her would've probably caused too much attention. Instead, he jetted from the lot following Samuel, who was doing well over 80mph. I had some relief knowing my friend would be safe, but too bad I couldn't say the same for me.

Just when my mind finished processing my options, reality set in. Samuel pulled his pistol from his waist and set it slowly on the seat near his side. He seemed to be delusional, sorta in a scary daze.

I kept looking back, wishing someone was following us. A concerned stranger, the DEA, anybody...I didn't care who it was. I gave a sigh of relief when I saw Lou's car turn off. At least they weren't gonna gang rape me or some shit. I prayed and thanked the Lord.

The car was so silent, I was afraid to even move in my seat. I tried to look straight ahead, not wanting to look him in the eye. I wondered where we were going, but couldn't bring myself to ask. When we got on Interstate 20, I prayed he'd at least dump my body where someone would find me. It was almost as if I knew I would die tonight.

By the time I finished praying, and shedding my tears, which obviously didn't affect Samuel, we'd pulled into his neighborhood. I thought, *what the hell is going on? Why is he taking me to his house?*

When he pulled into the garage, I instantly noticed my car wasn't there. "Where the fuck is my car?" I said, quietly under my breath. I wondered if he'd sold it or even worse-given it to some bitch?

Quickly, Samuel pressed the button on his portable garage opener, bringing me one step closer to being trapped inside. When the door shut completely, he hopped out, ran toward my side of the car, and snatched open the car door. Before I knew it, he tugged at my shoulders with force, and practically dragged me from the car by my hair. I screamed at the pain, yet the feel of his gun rubbing against my leg scared me even more.

Once inside, he dragged me straight to the kitchen, and

threw me up against the counter with a struggle. Samuel stepped back nearly a yard from me, and looked me up and down intensely. Our eyes locked when I lifted my head. Shame infiltrated my body.

"How the fuck could you do this to me?" he winced.

I was speechless.

"Answer me!" he yelled. "How could you play me like that!"

"I...don't know what you're talking about. All I ever did was love you, baby," I said, with my arms in the air, welcoming him in.

Samuel looked like he wanted me to grab him by the arms and save him from the terrible mistake he was about to make. His eyes told me he wanted me, mentally and sexually.

"Didn't I always make you feel good, Samuel? I mean...you said my loving was the best you'd ever had." I pleaded with him... "Don't do this! Don't you remember how you felt inside of me?"

I figured if I could seduce him, or have him think back to the good times we had, or the way I made him feel, maybe he'd reconsider. After all, I *was* a real woman.

Samuel gave off a heavy sigh. He seemed to be considering my advance. I hoped. He moved closer toward my welcoming embrace.

As I took two steps closer, I called out to him, "Drop the gun baby. Let's talk about this. I promise I'll make it all better."

His face softened as he got up close in my face. Within seconds, my arms touched his warm skin, as he lifted his arms and knocked me vigorously in the head with the butt of his pistol.

My arms rose higher trying to block the powerful hits, but to no avail, Samuel continued pistol whipping me right in the middle of his kitchen. Blood splattered across the kitchen counter, while Samuel swung like a sadistic killer.

Finally, I came to the fretful reality that there was nothing I could do. I dropped my hands, and watched my life being taken away from me.

In Those Jeans

Chapter Twenty Two

Slowly, my fingers twitched in the darkness trying to regain a sense of feeling. They inched toward the right side of my face where I felt my deepest gash. My left eye had swollen so quickly, I was afraid to try and open it. At that moment, I vaguely remembered being pistol whipped and realized I was alive. Just scared to see what Samuel had done to me. I could feel blood trickling down the side of my face, and could taste it swirling around my mouth.

I realized I must've blacked out, 'cause when I finally-opened my eyes, the entire upper part of my mid-section was tied up, keeping me from moving around in the high-back office chair. The lights were on, contrary to what I'd thought, and my eyes scanned the room, until they fell on Samuel. He stood near the refrigerator like a proud abuser, and pointed his gun in my direction with a sinister grin.

A crazy grin.

A frightening grin.

With my hands tied tightly behind my back, I squirmed in my seat hoping I could loosen the ropes a little.

"You're not going anywhere Chanel. Oh, I meant Terrell," Samuel said, with rage in his voice. "So stop trying!"

"It's Chanel actually," I replied in a low tone.

"Shit, once a man always a fuckin man!"

I decided to ignore his last comment. "So, what are you planning on doing, Samuel?" I called out to him. I kept trying to move around, hoping for a miracle, but the ropes were tied securely.

Samuel gazed in my direction, just before making a clicking sound with his gun.

Oh, Lord. Help me Father, I thought. I felt like I was already dead. He slowly walked toward me resembling a wild maniac, while I made direct eye contact with the barrel of his gun.

"Why don't you just kill me already?" I moaned, while kicking in my seat.

My cuts burned deep, so deep I could barely handle the pain. I sobbed out loud wanting two bullets to the head, or anything to put me out of my misery.

It seemed as if my prayers had been answered 'cause the knock at the door startled Samuel and made me wanna cry. It was my only chance to survive. So, I had to let the person at the door know that Samuel's crazy-ass was about to kill me.

"You better not say a fuckin word," he warned.

Samuel took off toward the door with a gangster-like strut. A strut that I'd never seen in him before. His pistol waved from side to side, like he was ready to handle whatever beef awaited him at the door.

I could no longer see him, but heard his roar, "Who the fuck is it?"

Whatever the response was, Samuel didn't like it. I assumed it was a neighbor, a salesperson, or damn…maybe even Lou. But then again, why wouldn't he want to open the door if it was Lou?

He rushed back into the kitchen area, keeping his gun gripped in one hand, while fumbling with the rope behind my back. Something was up. He just wasn't telling me.

My attention swiftly got diverted when two loud pounds to the door sounded like the FEDS were coming in. Samuel released his hands from the ropes, pausing in awe as the front door swung wide open, almost simultaneously sending me into a frenzy.

While Samuel fled to the kitchen cabinet, my mind raced, trying to figure out what the hell he was doing. The moment he opened the cabinet, a box of bullets fell to the floor, scattering about.

Fuck being quiet now, this niggs is about to kill me, I thought. "Help!"

Suddenly, movement in my peripheral vision startled me. I could see someone sliding up against the wall leading to the kitchen. He had his gun drawn, scaring the hell outta me. He moved with caution, shouting, "Police!"

The officer had no idea how happy I was to hear him say that. From the street clothes he wore, I thought for sure he was on Samuel's team.

When our eyes locked, the officer seemed to want answers from me, but he obviously saw that I was trapped, unable to move. I figured he needed to know where Samuel's crazy-ass was, so I nodded in his direction.

By that time, another officer shouted my name from the front of the house. I thought, *how the hell do they know my name?*

I watched as Samuel squatted on the floor searching for an escape from the kitchen. Worry filled his face, 'cause he and I both knew the kitchen sat toward the back of the house, and the only way out was a damn James Bond escape, which was out the window

Seconds passed. Then sirens were heard. Obviously, back up was on the way. I guess I felt like there was a chance that I'd be saved, I hollered, "Help me, please he's got a gun!"

Samuel looked at me in shock, trying to understand why I had developed so much courage or better yet why I was such a snitch. Just as he turned around, with the intent of shutting me up, a thin officer, who appeared to be in his twenties snuck him good, with his gun pointed, only two feet away. Surrounded, Samuel's eyes twitched, followed by a deranged movement.

"Drop your weapon!" the thin officer yelled.

Samuel stood tall, like he'd rather die than give in. The scene was becoming all too scary for me. I wanted to be free, but I also wanted Samuel to live. I kicked my feet in a fury, trying to gain some attention, and to my surprise, it worked.

My distraction sent the men wild.

Yells and screams all of a sudden infiltrated the room. Shouting blared from all directions, one demand after another. Although the officers had instructed Samuel to slowly drop his weapon, he kept his eyes on me, never obeying their demands.

"Drop your weapon!" a shout came from behind me.

I wasn't quite sure how many officers were in the house, but it seemed like a slew of voices. I closed my eyes tightly, 'cause Samuel was about to get done.

I screamed, "Samuel, put the gun down! They're gonna kill you!"

I listened as another officer repeated my words.

Samuel never released his pistol, but sat kneeling on the floor, while officers continued to shout from different sides of the room.

One brave, heavyset officer darted behind me, and reached to loosen my ropes. Just about the same time, Samuel finally lowered his gun, ready to give in...or so I thought.

Seconds later, he lifted his gun slightly. "You played me," he said, looking in my direction. When our eyes met, I wanted to say thank you for allowing me to live, but a gunshot to the neck pierced Samuel right below the chin.

I screamed out loud, just as three officers rushed Samuel to the floor.

"He was gonna drop his weapon!" I yelled. It seemed

like a mini-swat team had swarmed the house.

Instantly, I was taken out of the kitchen area, guided by another plain clothes officer as they carried Samuel in the opposite direction.

"You're a lucky woman, Ms. Martinez. You are Ms. Martinez, aren't you?" he questioned, to be sure.

I nodded.

"Well, we only came here to question you about a friend of yours who's been reported missing. Essence," he said slowly.

A lump formed in my throat. I tried to act both surprised and distraught, at the same time. I started limping even more as he guided me through the front door. I needed him to feel sorry for me.

The paramedics swarmed the front lawn, amongst all the other service workers. I thought they were all for Samuel, until the detective called out. "She needs some help over here."

Just as I watched a few EMT's head my way, I spotted Stacy through the crowd. She'd been held back by a stout looking officer, who was now letting her make a run for me. Strangely on her heels, was Pastor Joe Scott.

"You need medical attention, so I'll meet up with you at the hospital," my detective stalker announced, just as Stacy and Joe got within listening distance.

"Why are you going? I asked softly. "I haven't the slightest idea where Essence is."

"We just have a few questions for you, like when was the last time you saw her? This is normal when we're investigating a missing person. You know, some of her friends think she's dead. Murdered possibly."

Pastor Joe interrupted. "Listen, maybe I should be the one coming down to the station."

"Is this so?" the detective asked, pulling out a hand-sized spiral pad.

"The day before she was reported missing, I overheard Essence and Lou, Samuel's friend, arguing on the phone. Just to make sure she was okay, I jumped in my car and headed to her house, where I saw Lou coming out of her place. I just assumed all was well and they'd settled their dispute. But when I walked to her apartment and rang the bell, there was no answer. I still didn't think nothing of it, until she didn't answer my calls for days after."

"Ummmmmm. Yes, I'll certainly need you to come down to the station. And how do you know Essence, Sir?"

"I'm her Pastor. Anyway, I need to mention one last thing. This young lady here," he said, pointing to me, as they were lifting me into the ambulance on the stretcher. "She packed up and left Essence's place the night before the Lou incident. I picked her up myself."

"And you'll testify if need be to all that you've said so far."

"Of course. I'm a Pastor."

Pastor Joe Scott, my crazy, weird lover and friend shot me a wink, as I watched from inside the ambulance.

"Okay. Well Ms. Martinez, if we need you, we'll be in touch," he yelled, as if I couldn't hear him inside the ambulance. He moved a little closer to the doorway and paused. "I guess you know not to leave town, right?"

"She knows," Stacy interrupted.

"Don't worry Chanel, I'll tell them everything they need to know. You go get yourself looked at," Pastor Scott informed.

At that moment, Stacy ran over to give Pastor Scott a hug and thanked him for everything, before jumping in the back of the ambulance with me.

As the doors shut, and the ambulance pulled off, Stacy said she saw Samuel being led from the house in a stretcher. I asked her was he dead.

She replied, "Shit, not a chance."

On the ride to the hospital, Stacy revealed that she'd called Pastor Scott, after Samuel fled with me in the car. They took a shot at swinging past the house, just to see if he took me to the home we once shared. Thank God, they were right 'cause when they saw officers out front, they decided to tell them I'd been kidnapped by my husband. Once they found out the officers were there just to question me, they told them the whole story. I guess Samuel gave it away coming to the door looking deranged when they knocked.

"I still can't believe you called Pastor Scott to help you," I said to Stacy. I shook my head as much as I could without the pain increasing.

"Shiiiiid…I called everybody I could think of. And everyone who's ever known you," she chuckled. "I was worried about you, baby girl," she said in a more serious tone.

Although I was beat up, and my weave felt like it was hanging on by a piece of thread, I smiled because I was gonna live. And living life to the fullest was what I planned on doing. *Fuck Samuel*, I laughed to myself. *You can't keep a good girl down!*

Epilogue

Two weeks later I'd finally been released from the hospital. Although all my bandages had been removed from my face, my scars would be a constant reminder of the life I wanted to live with Samuel. A reminder of the pain and abuse he'd inflicted on me. As the nurse rolled me from my room to the front door, I watched Stacy's fine-ass waving from outside the double doors.

Although we hadn't made it outside yet, the sun shone brightly putting a smile on my face. The three days of rain had been wiped away just like the chaos in my life. A new start was what I needed.

The police had been to see me several times, each time losing more ground on their investigation. A pastor's word was golden to them, especially since Essence's body hadn't been found.

The fact that Pastor Scott gave his testimony, which all made sense, and didn't include me, cleared me for now. The police, however, did instruct me not to leave town, in case some evidence surfaced, and I needed to be questioned again. I'd already decided that as soon as I made some money, I'd be on the first thing smoking out of Atlanta.

I had enough of Hotlanta. My eyes were set to look for the next hot guy in the next city; one who would love me for me. Huh, I laughed. Who was I kidding? I'd never tell a man my secret. And this time…I'd be more careful about my meds, my past, and anything else that would ever give me away. Hell, I deserved to be married.

226

At that moment, I thought about Ray, my FedEx boo, who I'd called yesterday to let him know we would hook up soon. This time giving him my real name.

My attention shifted as soon as my wheelchair rolled over the over-sized welcome mat that read Newton General Hospital. My eyes nearly popped from my head. Stacy stood there smiling, ready to jump up and down.

I wasn't sure how to react. I thought about leaping from my wheelchair to give my mother a hug. Although she stood stiff, her eyes welcomed me.

"Ma, what are you doing here?"

"I'm here for you, Chanel."

Chanel, I thought. *Damn, she called me Chanel.*

Before I could say anything else, my mother rushed to my side and helped me from the wheelchair into what I assumed was a rental car. I didn't feel that bad, just stiff near my head, with a consistent headache. I sat in the backseat waiting like a helpless person for Stacy to stop talking to my mom outside the car once my door shut.

What are they talking about, I wondered.

It didn't take long for Stacy to re-open my door, giving me a weird look. She bent down low, gripping her knees lightly.

"Girl, hop in," I said in a sassy tone.

"I'm not going where you're going. But I'm surely coming to visit you soon."

My forehead creased. "What do you mean?" I asked Stacy, but looking toward my mother, who leaned over the drivers seat, staring me in the face. "Okay…somebody tell me something. Whats going on?"

"Your safety," my mother answered.

"Look, I'll let your mother explain. Just know that I've got somebody waiting to go with me to my place to move out. Thanks to my good friend here," she looked toward my mother, "I've got a little cash now, so, I'm moving on. Maybe even meeting up with you in another state."

"What the hell!" I shouted, with complete shock.

"Look, don't worry. We are friends for life," she said, grabbing my hand tightly.

I wanted to snatch my hand back, but decided to allow my palm to rest comfortably inside of hers. Her hands were warm and soothing. After all, she was my best friend, and the only person who made me feel one hundred percent comfortable about myself.

"Love ya, girl. I'll be in touch."

Stacy kissed me on my cheek and shut the door. As soon as my mother pulled off, making me feel as if she were my chauffer, she started explaining things that I wanted to ask her. When she told me that she left my father, my face tightened a bit, causing me pain.

"I should've done it years ago," she said, in a shameful voice.

I figured my silence would give her a chance to finish.

"I knew all along," she cried. "I just pray the Good Lord will forgive me. And you too." Her arms struggled to turn the wheel, making a u-turn out of the parking lot. "I was afraid. I didn't know what to do."

My mother's tears made for a heart-wrenching scene. Although I'd been the victim, my heart went out for her.

"You were my son, and I didn't protect you. I'm sorry," she mumbled. "I wanted to turn him in. I really did…"

"Momma, say no more. I understand. He's scared me all my life. Where will you go?" I leaned forward to ask. I placed my hand on her right shoulder to let her know I was with her, and loved her too.

Her sniffles slowed as she regained composure. "Well, I'm starting a new life. And so are you. When Stacy called and told me all that happened, I knew it was my chance to do some good in your life."

She grabbed a mid-sized packing envelope from her purse. The rubber bands tied tightly had me wondering what sat inside.

"There's enough money in there for you to start a new life. I know the police said don't leave town, but you gotta go. You need to be away from Samuel. Away from danger.

Damn, Stacy must've told her everything. She knows about the police saying don't leave town…and all about Samuel.

We talked for the next twenty minutes about my mode of transportation for leaving town. One thing became certain. First thing in the morning, I would kiss Atlanta goodbye, and my mother was never going back to my father. I bowed my head low and prayed. I thanked God for giving me life. I thanked God for saving my life. And I thanked God for my mother. *Oh, and Lord…wherever I end up, please send me a good looking man.*

Meet Mirror Carter, a hood chick from Shady Grove Trailer Park who would die to forget her past, and bask in a more sophisticated lifestyle. Although Mirror gets a small taste of the glamorous life, her appetite for wealth continues to grow as she constantly searches for the next big money-maker. That is until she meets, Brice Tower; the handsome, and filthy rich owner of the Houston Rockets, and her meal ticket to the millionaire's club.

Soon, chaos erupts and Mirror's fairy-tale life turns into a nightmare when she finds out Brice's best kept secret. As Mirror vows to hold on to her spot at the top, Brice struggles to keep her away. When the game of fatal attraction turns hood, Mirror's past is exposed and all hell breaks lose.

IN STORES NOV '08

Womanizer, Antoine Moore believed that women were only good for one thing...*lying on their backs*. However, the professional bachelor's wild exotic journeys are brought to a halt, when one of his former flings, leaves their daughter, Angel on his door step. Forced to raise her, he struggles to balance fatherhood and his passion for women. Antoine quickly realizes Angel's ability to attract the opposite sex, so he deviously uses her as bait. As Angel develops into a sexy young lady and begins to display Antoine's destructive behavior, she heads to the streets using the only thing she can ... *her body*. When Angel's life spins out of control and her twisted perception of love continues, Antoine is determined to change his ways. Will his decision to finally transform from a boy to a man save his number one girl when a devastating secret from the past is revealed?

IN STORES NOW!

Hot Headed and Hot Blooded

Marina Maxwell, a successful news anchor in Atlanta, has had anger issues with men since high school. But, she believes she can calm her fiery temper once the right man comes into her life. In walks tall and handsome Mangus Baskerville, a police officer who's feeling her so tough that he quickly proposes marriage. Yet once the I Do's are exchanged, Mangus discovers the other side of Marina . . . a side that is flawed through anger. Can Mangus stand by his abusive woman even when the other woman lurks nearby? And can Marina learn to mellow her violent ways just in time?

PICK UP A COPY TODAY

Where There's Smoke.....There's FIRE!!!

What happens when your man walks out on you for the other younger woman? Lovett Anderson a.k.a. Love cradled the idea of Home Sweet Home, while her cheating fiancé' Chase provided only a mirage. Being defeated in a fight to the death with his mistress, she's left abandoned, scorned and contemplating suicide. Finally finding a safe haven with close friends, Love gets the strength to live again moving her into the arms of her new dream man. Reluctant and still struggling with her hidden past and torn emotions, Love's new mate ignites flames of fury and they sketch out the perfect plan of revenge. Tightly concealed deceptions reveal painful truths in this gripping and heart wrenching story. Watch who you rub the wrong way because the **FRICTION** could be deadly!

Visit Nicolette at: www.myspace.com/paperdollthebook

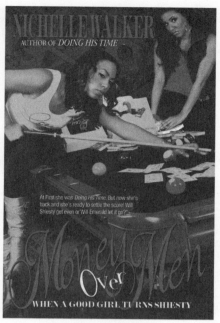

MAIL TO:

PO Box 423
Brandywine, MD 20613
301-362-6508

FAX TO:

301-579-9913

ORDER FORM

Ship to:	
Address:	
City & State:	Zip:
Attention:	

Date:	
Phone:	
E-mail:	

Make all checks and money orders payable to: **Life Changing Books**

Qty.	ISBN	Title	Release Date	Price
	0-9741394-0-8	A Life To Remember by Azarel	Aug-03	$ 15.00
	0-9741394-1-6	Double Life by Tyrone Wallace	Nov-04	$ 15.00
	0-9741394-5-9	Nothin Personal by Tyrone Wallace	Jul-06	$ 15.00
	0-9741394-2-4	Bruised by Azarel	Jul-05	$ 15.00
	0-9741394-7-5	Bruised 2: The Ultimate Revenge by Azarel	Oct-06	$ 15.00
	0-9741394-3-2	Secrets of a Housewife by J. Tremble	Feb-06	$ 15.00
	0-9724003-5-4	I Shoulda Seen It Comin by Danette Majette	Jan-06	$ 15.00
	0-9741394-4-0	The Take Over by Tonya Ridley	Apr-06	$ 15.00
	0-9741394-6-7	The Millionaire Mistress by Tiphani	Nov-06	$ 15.00
	1-934230-99-5	More Secrets More Lies by J. Tremble	Feb-07	$ 15.00
	1-934230-98-7	Young Assassin by Mike G.	Mar-07	$ 15.00
	1-934230-95-2	A Private Affair by Mike Warren	May-07	$ 15.00
	1-934230-94-4	All That Glitters by Ericka M. Williams	Jul-07	$ 15.00
	1-934230-93-6	Deep by Danette Majette	Jul-07	$ 15.00
	1-934230-96-0	Flexin & Sexin by K'wan, Anna J. & Others	Jun-07	$ 15.00
	1-934230-92-8	Talk of the Town by Tonya Ridley	Jul-07	$ 15.00
	1-934230-89-8	Still a Mistress by Tiphani	Nov-07	$ 15.00
	1-934230-91-X	Daddy's House by Azarel	Nov-07	$ 15.00
	1-934230-87-1-	Reign of a Hustler by Nissa A. Showell	Jan-08	$ 15.00
	1-934230-86-3	Something He Can Feel by Marissa Montelih	Feb-08	$ 15.00
	1-934230-88-X	Naughty Little Angel by J. Tremble	Feb-08	$ 15.00
	0-9741394-9-1	Teenage Bluez	Jan-06	$ 10.99
	0-9741394-8-3	Teenage Bluez II	Dec-06	$ 10.99
			Total for Books	$
		Shipping Charges (add $4.25 for 1-4 books*)		$
		Total Enclosed (add lines)		$

* **Prison Orders-** Please allow up to three (3) weeks
for delivery.

For credit card orders and orders over 25 books, please
contact us at orders@lifechaningbooks.net
(Cheaper rates for COD orders)

*Shipping and Handling of 5-10 books is $6.25, please
contact us if your order is more than 10 books. (301)362-
6508